Then

Morris Gleitzman grew up in England and went to live in Au[s]
when he was sixteen. He worked as a frozen-chicken thaw[er]
sugar-mill rolling-stock unhooker, fashion-industry trainee,
department-store Santa, TV producer, newspaper columnist and
screenwriter. Then he had a wonderful experience. He wrote a novel
for young people. Now he's one of the bestselling children's authors
in Australia. He lives in Melbourne, but visits Britain regularly.
His many books include *Two Weeks with the Queen*, *Water Wings*,
Bumface, *Boy Overboard* and *Once*.

Visit Morris at his website:
morrisgleitzman.com

Books by Morris Gleitzman

Then

MORRIS GLEITZMAN

PUFFIN

PUFFIN BOOKS

Published by the Penguin Group
Penguin Books Ltd, 80 Strand, London WC2R 0RL, England
Penguin Group (USA) Inc., 375 Hudson Street, New York, New York 10014, USA
Penguin Group (Canada), 90 Eglinton Avenue East, Suite 700, Toronto, Ontario, Canada M4P 2Y3
(a division of Pearson Penguin Canada Inc.)
Penguin Ireland, 25 St Stephen's Green, Dublin 2, Ireland (a division of Penguin Books Ltd)
Penguin Group (Australia), 250 Camberwell Road, Camberwell, Victoria 3124, Australia
(a division of Pearson Australia Group Pty Ltd)
Penguin Books India Pvt Ltd, 11 Community Centre, Panchsheel Park, New Delhi – 110 017, India
Penguin Group (NZ), 67 Apollo Drive, Rosedale, North Shore 0632, New Zealand
(a division of Pearson New Zealand Ltd)
Penguin Books (South Africa) (Pty) Ltd, 24 Sturdee Avenue, Rosebank, Johannesburg 2196,
South Africa

Penguin Books Ltd, Registered Offices: 80 Strand, London WC2R 0RL, England

puffinbooks.com

First published in Australia by Penguin Group (Australia),
a division of Pearson Australia Group Pty Ltd 2008
First published in Great Britain by Puffin Books 2009
014

Text copyright © Creative Input Pty Ltd, 2008
All rights reserved

The moral right of the author has been asserted

Set in 13 Minion
Made and printed in England by Clays Ltd, St Ives plc

British Library Cataloguing in Publication Data
A CIP catalogue record for this book is available from the British Library

ISBN: 978-0-141-32482-1

www.greenpenguin.co.uk

MIX
Paper from
responsible sources
FSC® C018179

Penguin Books is committed to a sustainable
future for our business, our readers and our planet.
This book is made from Forest Stewardship
Council™ certified paper.

For all the children
who have to hide

Then we ran for our lives, me and Zelda, up a hillside as fast as we could.

Which wasn't very fast.

Not even with me holding Zelda's hand and helping her up the slope.

You know how when you and two friends jump off a train that's going to a Nazi death camp and you nearly knock yourself unconscious but you manage not to and your glasses don't even get broken but your friend Chaya isn't so lucky and she gets killed so you bury her under some ferns and wild flowers which takes a lot of strength and you haven't got much energy left for running and climbing?

That's how it is now for me and Zelda.

'My legs hurt,' says Zelda.

Poor thing. She's only six. Her legs aren't very big. And she's wearing bedtime slippers which aren't very good for scrambling up a steep hill covered with prickly grass.

But we can't slow down.

We have to get away before another Nazi train comes along with machine guns on the roof.

I glance over my shoulder.

At the bottom of the hill, the railway track is gleaming in the sun like the shiny bits on a Nazi officer's uniform.

I peer up the slope.

At the top is a thick forest. When we get up there we'll be safe. We'll be hidden. The next Nazi train won't be able to see us as long as Zelda doesn't yell rude things at them.

If we can get up there.

'Come on,' I say to Zelda. 'Keep going. We mustn't stop.'

'I'm not stopping,' says Zelda indignantly. 'Don't you know anything?'

I know why Zelda's cross. She thinks I'm lucky. I am. I'm ten. I've got strong legs and strong boots. But I wish my legs were stronger. If I was twelve I could carry Zelda on my back.

'Ow,' she says, slipping and bashing her knee.

Gently I pull her up.

'Are you OK?' I say.

'No,' she says as we hurry on. 'This hill is an idiot.'

I smile, but not for long.

Suddenly I hear the worst sound in the world. The rumble of another train in the distance, getting closer.

I peer up the slope again.

The forest is too far. We won't get there in time. If the Nazis see us on this hillside we'll be easy targets. My shirt's got rips in it that are flapping all over the place. Zelda's dress is lots of colours but not camouflage ones.

The train is getting very close.

'Lie flat,' I say, pulling Zelda down onto the grass.

'You said we mustn't stop,' she says.

'I know,' I say. 'But now we mustn't move.'

'I'm not moving,' says Zelda. 'See?'

We're lying on our tummies, completely still except for a bit of panting. Zelda is clinging on to me. Her face is hot against my cheek. Her hands are gripping my arm. I can see that one of her finger-nails is bleeding from pulling up ferns for Chaya.

The noise of the train is very loud now. Any second it'll be coming round the bend below us. I wish we had ferns to hide under. Near us is a rabbit hole. I wish me and Zelda were rabbits. We could crouch deep in the hillside and eat carrots.

But we're not, we're humans.

The Nazi train screeches round the bend.

Zelda grips me even tighter.

'Felix,' she says. 'If we get shot, I hope we get shot together.'

I feel the same. I squeeze her hand. Not too tight because of her fingernail.

I wish we were living in ancient times when

machine guns were really primitive. When you'd be lucky to hit a mountain with one even up close. Instead of in 1942 when machine guns are so super-modern they can smash about a thousand bullets into an escaping kid even from the top of a speeding train.

Below us the Nazi train is clattering like a thousand machine guns.

I put my arm round Zelda and pray to Richmal Crompton to keep us safe.

'Zelda isn't Jewish,' I tell Richmal Crompton silently. 'But she still needs protection because Nazis sometimes kill Catholic kids too. Specially Catholic kids who are a bit headstrong and cheeky.'

Richmal Crompton isn't holy or anything, but she's a really good story-writer and in her books she keeps William and Violet Elizabeth and the other children safe even when they're being extremely headstrong and cheeky.

My prayer works.

No bullets smash into our bodies.

'Thank you,' I say silently to Richmal Crompton.

Down the hill I see the train disappearing round the next bend. I can tell it's another death camp train full of Jewish people. It's got the same carriages our train had, the ones that look like big wooden boxes nailed shut.

On the roof of the last carriage there's a machine gun, but the two Nazi soldiers sitting behind it are busy eating.

'Come on,' I say to Zelda as soon as the train is out of sight.

We get to our feet. At the top of the hill the forest waits for us, cool and dark and safe.

I don't know how long till the next train, so we have to move fast. We might not be so lucky with the next one. The Nazi machine gun soldiers might not be having an early dinner.

I grab Zelda's hand and we start scrambling up the slope again.

Zelda trips on a rabbit hole and almost falls. I save her but accidentally almost yank her arm out of its socket.

'Sorry,' I say.

'It's not your fault,' says Zelda. 'It's the rabbits' fault. Don't you know anything?'

She lets go of my hand and holds her shoulder and her dark eyes fill with tears.

I put my arms round her.

I know her shoulder isn't the only reason she's crying. It's also because of what's happened to our parents and our friends. And because the most powerful army in the history of the world is trying to kill us.

If I start thinking about all this I'll end up crying myself.

Which is not good. People who are crying can't climb hillsides very fast. I've seen it happen.

I try to think of a way to cheer us both up.

'In the next valley there might be a house,' I say.

'With a really kind cook. Who's made too much dinner and who's looking for people to help eat the extra platefuls of delicious stew.'

'Not stew,' says Zelda. 'Sausages.'

'OK,' I say. 'And boiled eggs.'

'And marmalade,' says Zelda. 'On bread fingers.'

It's working. Zelda has stopped crying. Now she's pulling me up the hill.

'And bananas,' I say.

'What's bananas?' says Zelda.

While we climb I tell her about all the exotic fruit I've read about in stories. That's another way I'm lucky. I grew up in a bookshop. Zelda didn't, but she's still got a really good imagination. By the time we get to the top of the hill, she's fairly certain the cook has got mangoes and oranges for us as well.

We plunge into the forest and hurry through the thick undergrowth. It feels really good to be in here with the ferns and bushes and trees sheltering us. Specially when I suddenly hear a scary sound in the distance.

Machine guns.

We stop and listen.

'Must be another train,' I say.

We look at each other. The machine guns go on and on, not close but still terrifying.

I don't say anything about train people trying to escape, in case they're getting shot dead. There's only so much getting shot dead a little kid like Zelda can take.

'Do you want to rest?' I say to her.

What I actually mean is does she want to hide, but I don't say that either because I don't want her to feel even more scared.

'No,' says Zelda, pushing ahead. 'I want my dinner.'

I know how she feels. Better to get further away from the railway line. Plus it's almost evening and we haven't eaten all day.

I follow her.

At last the distant shooting stops.

'The house is this way,' says Zelda, scrambling through a tangle of creepers.

That's the good thing with stories. There's always a chance they can come true. Poland is a big country. It's got a lot of Nazis in it, but it's also got a lot of forests. And a lot of houses. And quite a few sausages.

'Has the cook got chocolate?' says Zelda after a while.

'Maybe,' I say. 'If we think about it really hard.'

Zelda screws up her forehead as we hurry on.

By the time we get to the other side of the forest, I'm pretty sure the cook has got chocolate, a big bar of it.

We pause at the edge of the trees and squint down into the next valley. My glasses are smudged. I take them off and polish them on my shirt.

Zelda gives a terrified squeak, and grabs me and points.

I put my glasses back on and peer down at what she's seen.

Zelda isn't pointing at a distant house belonging to a kind cook, because there aren't any houses. She's pointing at something much closer.

A big hole in the hillside. A sort of pit, with piles of freshly dug earth next to it. Lying in the hole, tangled up together, are children. Lots of them. All different ages. Some older than me, some even younger than Zelda.

'What are those children doing?' says Zelda in a worried voice.

'I don't know,' I say.

I'm feeling worried too.

They look like Jewish children. I can tell because they're all wearing white armbands with a blue blob that I'm pretty sure is a Jewish star.

Trembling, I give my glasses another clean.

'This wasn't in your story,' whispers Zelda.

She's right, it wasn't.

The children aren't moving.

They're dead.

That's the bad thing with stories. Sometimes they don't come true and sometimes what happens instead is even worse than you can imagine.

I try to stop Zelda seeing the blood.

Too late.

She's staring, mouth open, eyes wide.

I go to put my hand over her mouth in case she makes a noise and the killers are still around.

Too late.

She starts sobbing loudly.

Directly below us on the hillside, several Nazi soldiers jump to their feet in the long grass. They glare up the hill towards us. They throw away their cigarettes and shout at us.

I know I should get Zelda back into the undergrowth, out of sight, but I can't move.

My legs are in shock.

The Nazi soldiers pick up their machine guns.

Then the Nazi soldiers started shooting at us and suddenly I could move again.

And think.

Grab Zelda.

Get away.

Hide.

Bullets are cracking into the tree trunks all around us. Bits of flying bark are stinging us in the face.

We turn and run back into the forest, jumping over logs, crashing through bushes, weaving around brambles, slithering in and out of tangled under-growth, scrambling over rocks.

I try not to think about Zelda's poor feet in their bedtime slippers or about the poor dead children in their pit.

Hide.

'Over there,' I say to Zelda. 'That big clump of bushes.'

We wriggle under thorny branches and through thick layers of ivy. With my hands I dig down into last year's leaves, which are damp and soft and even a bit warm when you get deep enough.

Zelda digs too and doesn't complain once about her sore finger.

We don't stop until we've made a secret place that is dark and quiet where we lie trembling and listening.

Zelda holds my hand.

I can hear Nazi soldiers shouting. Their boots are thudding as they run around in the forest looking for us. Nazi dogs are barking.

You know how when you're living in a secret cellar in a city ghetto with lots of other kids and you all make a tent with your coats and snuggle inside and try to feel cosy and safe even though outside the streets are full of Nazis?

That's what me and Zelda are doing in this burrow, except we haven't got our coats any more.

We haven't got our friends from the cellar either. I say a silent prayer to Richmal Crompton. I ask her to protect our friends who are still on that terrible train. Please don't let them end up in a pit too.

Suddenly, thinking about that makes me not want to stay cosy and safe in this hole.

I want to jump out and find a sharp stick and creep up on those Nazis and stab them hundreds of times until their guts are hanging out and they beg for mercy and promise never to shoot people ever again. But I wouldn't show them mercy, I'd keep stabbing them and stabbing them and –

'You're hurting me,' whispers Zelda.

I realise I'm squeezing her hand really tight.

'Sorry,' I say, letting go.

I don't tell her what I was thinking. She's seen enough killing and violence today without me going on about more.

I feel ashamed and push the angry thoughts out of my mind.

Zelda holds my hand again.

'It's OK,' she says. 'I'm frightened too.'

In the distance the soldiers are still shouting. I don't speak German, but you don't have to understand the words to know when somebody wants to kill you.

'Don't worry,' I whisper to Zelda. 'The Nazis won't find us.'

I hope I'm right.

I can't see Zelda in the gloom, but I know she's thinking about something. I can tell from her serious breathing in my ear.

'Felix,' she says at last. 'Those children who were shot. Where are their mummies and daddies?'

I have to wait a bit before I reply because just thinking about those children makes me feel very sad and upset. I try to imagine them covered up with ferns and wild flowers, but it doesn't help.

'I don't know,' I say quietly. 'I don't know

where their mummies and daddies are.'

It's the truth. They could be dead with bullets in them like Zelda's parents, or sent to a death camp like mine, or they could be alive and just discovering the terrible thing that's been done to their children.

I don't say these things out loud. Zelda is still trembling and I don't want to upset her even more.

'Did some Nazis make those children dead?' asks Zelda.

I hesitate again.

I know why she's asking.

'Probably,' I say. 'But we can't be certain. We didn't actually see them do it.'

Zelda's breathing is even louder now and I can tell she knows they did.

'I hate Nazis,' she says.

Poor thing. She must feel awful. Her mum and dad were Nazis before the Polish resistance killed them. I've seen the photo of her father in a Nazi uniform in the locket round her neck. When I think about my mum and dad being dead, at least I know they were Jewish and innocent. Poor Zelda has to think about her parents being part of a gang of brutal murderers.

'Your mummy and daddy loved you very much,' I say to her gently. 'Try to remember that.'

'I can't,' says Zelda.

'Try to think about a happy time you had with them,' I suggest.

It's what I do when I'm feeling bad about Mum and Dad, but it doesn't always work.

'When I was little,' says Zelda, 'we had chickens. Not Nazi chickens, nice chickens.'

She starts crying.

I try to think of something else to say. Something to help Zelda have happy memories of her parents. But I can't think of anything.

'I wish I was little now,' she sobs.

Poor thing. It must be terrible to not have a family when you're only six. It's bad enough when you're my age.

'You've still got a family,' I say quietly to Zelda.

I reach out in the darkness and give her a hug so she knows I mean me.

Zelda doesn't say anything, but she snuggles closer and cries into my shirt so I'm pretty sure she does know.

'Felix,' she says when she's finished crying. 'Will you always be my family?'

'Yes,' I say.

'Will you stay with me for ever and ever?' she says.

I think about this. I remember how Mum and Dad promised to come back one day and they never did. But I know they wanted to. That's the important thing with a promise. You must want to keep it.

'I promise,' I say.

'I promise too,' says Zelda.

She snuggles into me.

I listen for the soldiers again.

Nothing, just forest insects and the wind in the trees. But the Nazis might not have gone yet. They could be back at the pit, smoking more cigarettes and covering the children with dirt.

'I think we should hide here till morning,' I say to Zelda.

'All right,' she says.

'We haven't got any dinner,' I say. 'Sorry.'

There aren't even any weeds in this burrow, just old leaves. We daren't eat those in case there's mould on them that gets into our brains and makes us think we're opera singers. I've seen it happen.

'That's OK,' says Zelda in a small voice. 'I'm not hungry.'

I know she is because I am.

I hug her even tighter. Sometimes love from your family can make your tummy not hurt quite so much.

'Go to sleep,' I whisper to Zelda.

'Tell me a story,' she says. 'One where nobody gets dead.'

I tell her a story about two children called Felix and Zelda who meet two other children called William and Violet Elizabeth. They all live together with some very friendly chickens who give them lots of eggs to eat. To say thank you to the chickens, Felix and Zelda invent a machine that feeds them automatically.

'That's silly,' murmurs Zelda. 'Machines can't feed chickens.'

'It's in the future,' I say. '1965.'

'All right,' says Zelda.

Richmal Crompton doesn't set her William stories in the future, but I'm sure she wouldn't mind.

The wind in the trees is getting louder now and the air is getting colder. Carefully I scoop some more leaves onto Zelda to keep her warm.

'More story, please,' she murmurs.

'One of the chickens falls in love with Zelda,' I say. 'It wants to be her pet. She calls it Hubert.'

'Don't you know anything?' says Zelda sleepily. 'My pet chicken's name is Goebbels.'

'Sorry,' I say.

I tell her the next part of the story, about how Goebbels can juggle eggs.

Finally Zelda's soft breathing lets me know she's asleep.

I wish I could doze off too, but I can't. There are busy insects in these leaves and they tickle.

My brain is busy as well, wondering what we're going to do next. If we don't get food soon, we're in big trouble. There's not much point being snug and safe in a secret burrow if you're dead.

We need a safe hiding place that has food.

The only safe place I know in the whole of Poland that definitely has food is the Catholic orphanage where Mum and Dad hid me. But it's hundreds of kilometres away. We'd have to get past about a million Nazis to even find it.

Zelda's bedtime slippers just wouldn't last the distance. Neither would our tummies.

We need somewhere local.

Which means I'll have to ask a grown-up for help.

But asking for help can be risky these days. A lot of grown-ups aren't very good at listening to kids, specially not while they're shooting them.

Then I fell asleep and the next morning me and Zelda went to find some new parents.

Slowly.

Carefully.

Watching out for Nazis.

'Why?' says Zelda sleepily, rubbing her eyes as we creep along the forest path. 'Why do we need new parents?'

'To keep us safe,' I tell her. 'To look after our sore fingers and give us breakfast.'

Zelda thinks about this. We're both shivering in the cool damp morning air. We haven't had anything to eat or drink for a whole day and two nights. I can see she likes the idea of a hot breakfast as much as I do.

While I keep my eyes peeled for Nazi soldiers in the undergrowth and Nazi dive-bombers above the trees, I tell her my plan.

She listens quietly.

But not for long.

'No,' she shouts, and plonks herself down at the side of the path.

I knew Zelda wouldn't like this part of the idea. The part that involves going back to the big hole with the dead children in it.

I don't like it either, but it's a vital and important part of the plan.

I try not to get irritated with Zelda. Hunger and thirst can make you really grumpy if you're not careful.

'You won't have to see the children,' I explain to her. 'They'll probably be covered up with earth. A grave is a really good place to meet new parents. If the mums and dads are still alive, sooner or later they'll want to visit the place where their kids are buried. And we'll be there, offering ourselves as replacements.'

Zelda frowns as she thinks about this.

I glance nervously around the forest. I'm hoping she'll agree it's a really good plan, but I'm also hoping she'll do it quietly.

'What does replacements mean?' says Zelda.

'Parents with dead kids sometimes adopt new ones,' I explain. 'It's no trouble for them, they've already got the bedrooms set up and everything.'

Zelda slowly stands up.

I can see she's starting to understand what a good idea this is.

But before she can tell me how grateful she is to

have such a clever family as me, there's a snapping and crackling nearby and something hurtles towards us out of the undergrowth.

For a panicked second I think it's a Nazi dog, one of those big vicious killer brutes trained to bite you even through your clothes.

I try to get between Zelda, who's cowering and whimpering, and the vicious killer brute.

Except now I can see it isn't a vicious killer brute.

It's another kind of dog, big and floppy and panting with untidy brown fur like an old armchair with the stuffing showing. And big sad eyes that stare up at me while it licks a bare bit of my tummy through a rip in my shirt.

'Stop that,' says Zelda sternly to the dog. 'It's rude to lick tummies.'

I don't mind. Mum used to lick my tummy when I was little.

The dog turns and starts licking Zelda's arm.

She stops frowning and starts chuckling.

I look around for the dog's owner. I have a feeling he or she probably isn't a Nazi, but you can't be too careful. Before I can spot anybody, a whistle echoes through the trees and the dog gives Zelda one last lick and runs off into the undergrowth.

I still can't see anybody.

'Pity,' I say to Zelda. 'A person who owns a dog like that is probably nice.'

Zelda thinks about this.

Suddenly she yells as loud as she can.

'Hey, dog man or dog lady. We're over here. Felix and Zelda. Two kids who need breakfast and a mummy and daddy.'

In a panic, I put my hand over Zelda's mouth. Every Nazi in Poland probably heard that.

Zelda pulls my hand away.

'I was going to say please,' she mutters, glaring.

Before I can remind her we're in a war zone, I hear more sounds coming through the trees.

Thudding sounds.

Rattling sounds.

Getting closer.

I grab Zelda and look frantically around for a hiding place in the ferns and creepers. Somewhere marching Nazi soldiers with machine guns won't spot us.

I see a place.

'Come on,' I hiss at Zelda.

She doesn't move. I love having her as my family, but sometimes I wish she wasn't so stubborn.

'Look,' she says pointing, her eyes going big.

I turn and look. Coming round a bend in the forest path is a wooden cart, rattling and squeaking, pulled by a plodding horse with thud-thudding hooves.

The driver is an old man.

I check to see if the nice dog is riding on the cart or running alongside. It doesn't seem to be.

The old man sees us and winks.

Zelda is still staring at him with big eyes.

'The kind cook,' she whispers.

He doesn't have oranges piled up in his cart, or chocolate. But he's got something almost as good. A huge mound of crisp fresh turnips. Suddenly I can taste them and I feel weak with hunger. Normally I don't like turnips, specially raw, but now the thought of that turnip juice running down my throat makes me desperate to have some.

The old man stops the cart.

I can't see the nice dog anywhere.

'You kids lost?' says the old man.

'No,' I say.

'Yes,' says Zelda. Right now she'll say anything for a turnip.

The man looks at us thoughtfully.

'Get on,' he says. 'I'll give you a lift.'

I hesitate.

'Where are you going?' I ask.

'To my farm,' says the man.

I think about this.

'Did you grow those turnips?' I say.

The man nods.

I put my arm round Zelda. I'm pretty sure the man isn't telling the truth about where he's going. I don't know much about farming, but where I come from if a person grows turnips on his farm, the reason he puts them in a cart is to take them to town. And in my experience towns are where Nazi soldiers have their headquarters.

22

'Actually,' I say, 'could we just have a turnip?'

'Or some sausages,' says Zelda.

The man smiles, but there's something a bit strange about the way he does it.

'Hop on,' he says. 'You can eat as much as you like on the way.'

Zelda starts to climb onto the cart.

The man reaches behind him and lifts her up. I step forward to pull her back down, but I'm so hungry I'm starting to feel dizzy and my tummy's making me have second thoughts.

Maybe we should go with the man. He might be telling the truth. He might be going back home to get something he's forgotten, like more turnips. He might give us stew and let us work for him and even offer to be our new parent or grandparent.

If he's lying, we can always jump off the cart and hide before we get to town.

I grab onto the side of the cart and begin to climb up after Zelda.

And stop.

Nailed to the side of the cart, right next to my face, is a tattered paper notice with printing on it. At the top is one word in big letters.

JEWS.

I read the rest of the notice.

Reward, it says. *For each Jew captured and handed over. Two hundred (200) zloty and one (1) bottle of vodka.*

Suddenly I'm not hungry any more. I'm thinking

clearly again. This is why the man wants to take us to town. To get a Nazi reward.

I drop back onto the ground.

'Zelda,' I yell. 'Jump off.'

Zelda glares down at me and shakes her head. Her cheeks are bulging and she's got mud and turnip juice round her mouth.

'Zelda,' I scream. 'It's a trap.'

The horse rears up. The old man swears at me. The cart lurches forward. The old man doesn't try to stop it. He obviously thinks one reward is better than nothing.

I run after the cart. The back flap is held in place by two big rusty metal pins. I grab them and twist them out. The flap drops and hundreds of turnips roll off the cart and knock me over.

Zelda rolls off the cart too.

'Ow,' she says as we lie on the ground with the turnips. She takes her knee out of my mouth. 'That hurts. Don't you know anything?'

I'm not thinking about knees, not even Zelda's hurting one. I'm thinking about the horrible thing I glimpsed in the cart, after the load started spilling and before my glasses got knocked off.

A boy, half-buried in turnips, not moving, covered in blood.

The old man must already have caught one Jewish kid today and bashed him unconscious and hidden him under the turnips.

The cart has stopped and the old man has

jumped down and is picking up turnips and yelling angrily at us. For a fraction of a second I wonder if I should try to rescue the boy.

No.

Get Zelda to safety.

You have to look after your family first. Plus the boy could already be dead.

I find my glasses and scramble up and grab Zelda's hand and drag her into the forest without looking back at the cart.

'Run,' I pant at her and we both do. We run until we're out of breath, which happens pretty quickly when you're weak from no food.

We flop to the ground behind a big tree. I'd like to be further away from the man, but I'm hoping he won't want to leave his cart in case somebody steals the Jewish boy to get the reward.

When my breathing quietens down, I listen carefully.

It doesn't sound like the man is following us.

'He wasn't a kind cook, was he,' whispers Zelda.

I shake my head.

'Sorry,' she says sadly. 'I didn't get you a turnip.'

'That's OK,' I say.

Looking at Zelda's kind concerned face, I feel a glow inside that makes the hunger seem not so bad.

'I know what we can do,' Zelda says. 'After the man's finished picking his turnips up and he's gone, we can go and see if he's missed one.'

'Good idea,' I say.

I don't tell her that no matter how hungry I am, I'm not sure if I could eat a turnip that's had blood on it.

Zelda gives me a hug.

'Thanks for saving me, Felix,' she says. 'I'm lucky to have you as my family.'

I'm about to tell her I'm lucky to have her as my family too, but I don't get the chance.

Twigs snap.

I try to spin round.

Too late.

'Run and you're dead,' says a gruff voice.

Strong hands grab us.

Then I knew me and Zelda were doomed. I knew what would happen next. We'd be bashed and thrown back onto the cart. Taken into town. Handed over to the Nazis. Made to lie down in a hole in the ground and ...

I was wrong.

You can be sometimes when your eyes are watering with hunger.

It's not the turnip man who's grabbed us, it's the dog lady.

I think she's a farmer too, judging by her clothes. And how strong she is. She's gripping my collar in one hand and there's no way I can get free. In her other hand she's got Zelda's arm and she's not letting go of that either, even though Zelda is trying to bite her on the finger.

'Stop that,' says the dog lady.

I stop wriggling. The big floppy dog is licking my tummy again. I look into its sad eyes. And at the friendly dribble hanging from its friendly mouth. This dog is definitely not a Nazi. Which means its owner probably isn't either.

I glance over at Zelda.

She's still wriggling.

'Kind farmer,' I mouth at her.

Zelda frowns. Either she doesn't understand what I'm saying, or she thinks I'm wrong.

I think I'm right. Now that I'm having a closer look at the woman, I can see she's got sad eyes like her dog. Her face isn't particularly friendly, but she's got the same sort of mouth as Mum, one that's kind at the corners. Her hair is shorter than Mum's though. You probably have to have short hair on a farm or the cows chew it. Mum was a bookseller so she didn't have that problem.

'Stop wriggling,' the woman snaps at Zelda.

'You're not the boss of me,' says Zelda fiercely.

'It's OK,' I say to Zelda. 'She's friendly.'

I'm wrong about that too.

'You stupid Jews,' says the woman.

I stare at her, not sure if I heard right.

'You yids are meant to be smart,' says the woman. 'I don't call staying around here smart. Not after what happened to your lot yesterday.'

I did hear right. Only people who hate Jews call us yids. Suddenly the woman's mouth doesn't look so kind after all.

'We don't want to stay around here,' I say. 'If you let go of us, we'll leave.'

The woman doesn't stop gripping my collar or Zelda's arm.

'Don't even think about it,' says the woman.

She starts pulling me and Zelda away through the forest. My collar is twisted and she's half choking me. She must know about the reward.

'You're hurting my arm,' says Zelda.

The woman ignores her.

Zelda finally manages to get her teeth into the woman's hand.

The woman lets go of my collar, slaps Zelda's face, and grabs my collar again before I can do anything.

Zelda cries.

The dog whimpers.

'I'm reporting you to the police,' I yell at the woman, but straight away I know that's a dumb thing to say because the police are all Nazis too.

The woman drags us both down another forest path. As we stumble along, I give Zelda a look to let her know I'm sorry I couldn't defend her. And that I'm trying to think what to do next.

The woman is too strong to fight. I used to think Mum and Dad were strong from lifting books, but this woman's got arm muscles like thick ropes.

'Listen,' I say to her. 'My parents have got thousands of books from their bookshop stored away. If you let us go, you can have them all. They're worth much more than four hundred zloty and two bottles of vodka.'

It's not true, but sometimes to try and save your family you have to make up stories.

'You Jews have certainly got imaginations,' says the woman.

She doesn't let us go.

'I'd probably do the same if I was an orphan,' she says. 'Make up lies about my parents.'

I look at the woman.

How does she know I'm an orphan?

Suddenly we all jolt painfully to a stop. Zelda has grabbed a tree trunk with her free arm and is clinging to it.

'We're not going with you,' she yells at the woman. 'You're horrible. You hurt people.'

The woman pulls Zelda away from the tree.

'And you're a naughty little girl,' she says angrily to Zelda, 'who by rights should be in that pit with your friends.'

She steers us along the forest path again, fast.

My brain is going fast too.

The woman thinks me and Zelda escaped from the group of children who got shot yesterday. That's why she's in such a hurry to take us to town. So she can hand us over to the Nazis and they can finish the job.

Desperately I try to think of another plan to get away.

Before I can, we come to the edge of the forest. It's a different place to where we were yesterday, with a different valley. I can tell because it doesn't have a children's grave. Just lots of farms. And in the distance I can see a town.

I can't see any Nazis in the town, but I know they're there.

Now I'm panicking.

I'm panting almost as hard as the dog.

Zelda is still crying. I don't blame her. Anyone would cry with a hurting arm and a hurting face both at once.

Suddenly I know what I have to do.

'Zelda's not Jewish,' I say to the woman. 'I am, but she's not. Take me, but let her go, please.'

I look at the woman pleadingly.

Zelda stops crying. She gives me a glare.

'Felix is wrong,' she says to the woman. 'I am Jewish.'

I can't believe it. Why is Zelda saying this? It's not true.

'Don't listen to her,' I say.

'I'm Jewish just like him,' Zelda says to the woman. 'I want to be Jewish and I am.'

I realise what Zelda's doing. She's saying this so we can stay together.

My head is bursting.

Doesn't Zelda realise staying with me could kill her? Has she forgotten about the poor children in the pit?

'Zelda's parents weren't Jewish,' I say frantically to the woman. 'Look at the photo in the locket round her neck. You'll see.'

31

We stop. Without letting go of my collar or Zelda's arm, the woman peers at Zelda's neck.

I do too.

The necklace with the locket isn't there.

'Where's the locket?' I shout at Zelda.

'I'm Jewish now,' she shouts back. 'You can't stop me.'

Suddenly I understand. Zelda must have left the locket in our burrow. So she doesn't have to think about her parents being Nazis.

I try to explain to the woman.

She's not listening.

'Both of you,' she says angrily. 'Be quiet.'

I give Zelda a look to let her know that the last thing I want is to be separated from her but I can't think of what else to do.

Zelda stares back at me, angry and hurt.

'You promised,' she says.

She's right, I did.

I feel terrible.

The woman marches us down into the valley, towards the town, towards the Nazis.

At least I can keep my promise now. Whatever happens next, at least it will happen to me and Zelda together.

Then the woman did a surprising thing. Instead of dragging me and Zelda into town and handing us over to the Nazis, she took us to a farm.

I think it's her farm.

You know how when you've been expecting something awful to happen and it doesn't, a field of cabbage stumps sparkling with morning dew can look even more beautiful than usual?

This field we're tramping through now looks like that.

My empty tummy gurgles with hope as the woman hurries us along the track towards a farmhouse.

Maybe she's a kind farmer after all.

OK, she's not exactly behaving like one. She's still gripping Zelda's arm very hard. I can tell from poor Zelda's face how much it hurts. And instead of dragging me by my shirt collar, she's dragging me by my left ear, which also hurts.

Why are we going so fast? We're almost trotting now. Zelda's little legs can hardly keep up.

'My feet hurt,' says Zelda.

Poor thing. They must hurt a lot. On the way here the woman marched us through a field of cut hay. The stubble frayed Zelda's bedtime slippers to bits. Her feet are bleeding.

'Stop complaining,' says the woman. 'We're nearly there.'

I should point out to the woman that Zelda is only six and is walking very fast for her age, but I can't get the words out. My throat is too dry and my mouth is too weak with hunger.

Only one thing is keeping me going.

The trickle of smoke coming out of the farm-house chimney.

Smoke can mean cooking. That might be why the woman is hurrying. And why the dog has rushed ahead and is barking at us. He might be letting us know that the sausage stew is done.

Just the thought of stew is giving me extra energy. Stew and boiled cabbage. I bet the cabbages on this farm are as beautiful as their stumps.

'Cooking,' I whisper to Zelda, pointing to the smoke so she can get extra energy too.

I notice something else very exciting about the farmhouse. It's got two windows. That means it's probably got two rooms. So if the woman lets us live with her, we won't be overcrowded and getting on her nerves all the time.

I send a silent message to Zelda.

Please don't bite the woman again. People don't invite you to live with them if you bite them.

Zelda doesn't bite the woman.

Even so, the woman doesn't invite us to live with her.

Instead we all stop outside a low barn built from lumps of stone. The woman lets go of my ear, takes a key from her trouser pocket, unlocks a big padlock and pulls the barn door open.

Several chickens rush out.

Zelda grins, which is pretty amazing for someone who's hungry and thirsty and in pain.

The woman doesn't grin. She pushes me and Zelda into the gloom.

'I don't want to hear a squeak,' she says sternly, and locks me and Zelda in.

For a long time we sit on a pile of straw, too worn out to speak.

Finally Zelda does.

'I know why that woman locked us in here,' she says.

I hope Zelda isn't thinking the same thing as me. That the woman couldn't be bothered dragging us all the way to town just for two bottles of vodka and four hundred zloty. So instead she's sent a message for the Nazis to come and get us.

'She did it as a punishment,' says Zelda. 'Because you broke your promise.'

I sigh, but I don't argue. It's better if Zelda isn't thinking about Nazis. She's too young to be hungry and thirsty and scared all at the same time.

'I'm sorry,' I say. 'I was just trying to protect you.'

'Leaving me isn't protecting,' says Zelda. 'Hiding me is protecting.'

'You're right,' I say. 'Let's hide now. Under the straw.'

It's our only hope. If the Nazis arrive and can't see us, maybe we'll have a chance to run for it.

We burrow deep into the straw.

'See?' says Zelda. 'This is good protecting.'

'We have to practise being very quiet,' I whisper.

'I don't need to practise,' she says. 'I'm good at being quiet. Don't you know anything?'

A loud snuffling fills the barn.

'Shhh,' I whisper.

'It's not me,' says Zelda.

The snuffling turns into wheezing.

Zelda grabs me.

It's dark in our hiding place and I can't see her, but I know she's thinking the same as me.

That we're not the only ones in this straw.

'Hello?' I whisper. 'Is anyone there?'

Maybe the farm woman has captured another Jewish person so she can get six hundred zloty and three bottles of vodka. Or maybe there's a Nazi soldier already here in the barn waiting for us.

I stop breathing.

The wheezing turns into grunting.

'That's not me,' whispers Zelda.

Suddenly there's a violent movement next to us and most of the straw isn't over us any more.

I blink in the faint haze of daylight coming under the barn door.

I'm staring up at a strange face. Two beady black eyes and a pink bald head and a big snout dripping with snot.

It's a pig.

'Naughty pig,' says Zelda. 'You're too noisy.'

The pig shuffles back a few steps.

'It's all right,' I say to Zelda. 'I think it's just lonely.'

I peer around the barn. I can't see any other pigs. I know I'd get lonely, stuck in a barn on my own all day without any family. With just a few chickens who don't even tell me when my nose is running.

I pat the pig.

Zelda grabs me. Outside, somebody is unlocking the barn door. We dive back into the straw. But before we can cover ourselves, the door swings open and the woman comes in. She puts a bowl of food onto the floor, and a bowl of water.

'Go on,' she says. 'Get it into you.'

I hesitate. Does she mean me and Zelda, or the pig?

The woman doesn't wait to explain. She steps out of the barn, slams the door shut and locks it again.

The pig doesn't wait either. It sticks its snout into the food and starts gobbling.

37

Me and Zelda hurry over and grab some.

The pig doesn't seem to mind.

'Thanks for sharing,' I say to the pig, my mouth full of delicious cold mashed potato and cabbage stalks.

'That's OK,' says Zelda.

Her mouth is so full her cheeks are bulging.

You know how when you're really hungry all you can think about is food, but as soon as you've eaten all you can think about is how thirsty you are?

That's happening to me.

I take my glasses off and stick my face in the water bowl and drink and drink.

Zelda does too.

So does the pig.

We all drink and drink and keep drinking until the Nazis arrive.

As soon as we hear the truck coming towards the farm, me and Zelda scramble back under the straw and make sure we're completely covered. Except for a tiny peephole so I can pick the right moment for us to run.

The barn door bangs open. I squint out through the straw. The woman comes in. She's wearing a dress now, and makeup, and she's brushed her hair. She takes a handful of something from her dress pocket and flings it around the barn.

What is she doing?

Outside the barn, men are yelling at each other

in Nazi and slamming the truck doors. Suddenly my nose tingles painfully and I know what the woman is scattering.

Pepper.

The woman wants me and Zelda to start sneezing so much we can't run. So we'll be helpless and the Nazi soldiers can grab us and she'll get her reward.

She's not a kind farmer, she's a horrible one.

Well, me and Zelda aren't going to sneeze. I press my fingers against my top lip and I press my other fingers against Zelda's.

'I can do it myself,' Zelda whispers indignantly, pushing my fingers away.

My hand brushes against something small and hard lying in the straw. I grab it. I can feel a chain. And a hinge. Zelda's locket. She must have had it in her pocket all the time. It must have fallen out when she was diving in and out of the straw.

I keep my eye at the peephole.

A Nazi soldier comes into the barn. He's got a rifle with a bayonet. A second soldier comes in with a dog. Not a floppy dog with sad eyes and comfy armchair fur. A vicious killer Nazi dog that's straining at its lead, desperate to bite people.

If it sniffs out me and Zelda, we're finished.

The Nazi dog coughs. The woman glances towards me and Zelda.

Oh no. I think she knows exactly where we are. She must have spotted our hiding place when she brought the food in.

It's too late to run. I squeeze the locket tight in my hand. When the woman drags us out of the straw and hands us over, I'm going to give the locket to the soldiers. When they see the photo of Zelda's father in Nazi uniform they'll have to show Zelda mercy.

Sometimes you have to break a promise if it's the only way to save your family.

That's weird. The woman isn't dragging us out and handing us over. She's standing very close to the soldiers, who are sniffing the air and frowning.

'Do you like it?' says the woman. 'My perfume?'

She gives them a cheeky grin, like Mum used to give Dad when she was up the ladder in the shop getting a book from the top shelf and Dad used to kiss her on the ankle.

The Nazi soldiers glance at each other.

The woman holds her wrist under their noses. They both sniff it. She gives them another cheeky grin. They both grin back.

I don't get it. If she wants to be romantic with Nazis, why doesn't she hand me and Zelda over first? That'll make them like her even more.

The Nazi dog sneezes.

Suddenly I have an amazing thought.

What if the pepper isn't for us? What if it's for the dog? What if the woman is doing some good protecting?

'Hope you find those two Jew kids,' says the

woman to the soldiers. 'So you can finish the job. I reckon the little vermin are hiding in the forest somewhere. You'll know them when you see them, they'll look like that.'

Chuckling, she points to the pig, who's in the corner, trembling, as far away from the Nazi dog as it can get.

The soldiers frown again. Is it because they don't like seeing an animal scared?

Probably not. It's probably because they don't speak much Polish.

Oh no.

The soldier with the rifle is coming over to where we're hidden. The woman looks like she wants to stop him, but she doesn't. The soldier stabs his bayonet into the pile of straw next to ours.

Should I jump out and show him the locket?

Too late, now he's raising his bayonet over our pile.

I want to put my arms round Zelda, but I daren't move. I pray she won't make a noise. I pray I won't either, not even if that bayonet slices into me.

Help us, Richmal Crompton, please.

The bayonet blade hisses into the straw just past my head. And again just near my chest. I can't see where it goes after that, but Zelda isn't making a sound.

The soldier stops stabbing.

He gives the woman a shrug and a grin. The woman stops biting her lip and gives a half-grin

41

back. But when the soldiers both turn away, she glances over towards me and Zelda again.

She looks very worried, like she really doesn't want us to be stabbed.

Yes.

My insides do a dance.

Except I'm feeling worried too.

Zelda still isn't making a sound.

The Nazi soldiers go out of the barn. The woman follows them. Just before she steps out the door, she forces a smile back onto her anxious face.

'Felix,' whispers Zelda in my ear. 'Are you stabbed?'

I've never been so happy to hear her voice.

'No,' I say.

'I'm not stabbed too,' says Zelda.

I put my arms round her and say a silent thank you to Richmal Crompton.

The Nazi soldiers are driving away. The woman is shouting friendly things after them, but I can tell she's only pretending.

Zelda's heart is going as fast as mine.

I'm not surprised.

It's pretty exciting when you get a new parent.

Then me and Zelda crawled out of the straw and the woman checked us over for stab wounds and was very relieved we didn't have any and took us into her house and gave us hot food including cabbage leaves and a whole turnip and a bath.

She also told us her name, which is Genia, and the dog's name, which is Leopold.

Zelda is first for the bath, but she doesn't want to get in.

'Come on, Zelda,' says Genia. 'This water won't stay hot for ever and I'm not heating any more.'

Zelda is staring at the kitchen floor, sticking out her bottom lip.

'You slapped me,' she says.

At first I can see Genia isn't sure what Zelda is talking about.

'In the forest,' says Zelda.

Now Genia remembers. She crouches down in front of Zelda.

'You bit me,' says Genia. 'So let's make a deal. If you don't bite me, I won't slap you.'

Zelda thinks about this.

She nods and gets into the bath. The deal works. Zelda doesn't bite Genia, and Genia is very gentle with Zelda's cut feet.

Now it's my turn.

My face is burning. Not from the water, because I'm standing up and it doesn't even reach my knees. My face is hot because Genia is staring at my private part like it's the most annoying thing she's ever seen.

I look away and pretend not to notice.

I was right about this house. It's got two rooms. There's the kitchen we're in now, and a completely separate bedroom. The house is made in a clever way. The wood stove is in the middle wall, so it heats both the rooms.

Genia is still staring at my private part.

Now she's sighing loudly.

'It's rude to stare,' says Zelda. 'Don't you know anything?'

'You Jews,' says Genia. 'Only Jews would do that to a kid.'

Of course. Now I know why she's staring. But it's not Mum and Dad's fault. They didn't want to have me circumcised.

'It wasn't my parents' fault,' I say to Genia. 'It was my grandfather. He was still alive when I was a baby and he made them do it. He said he'd get ill if they didn't do it.'

'Do what?' says Zelda.

'Chop off a perfectly good foreskin,' says Genia.

Now Zelda is staring at my private part too.

But only for a moment. She gives me the towel and a sympathetic look.

Genia isn't being sympathetic.

'What a very clever grandfather,' she says, taking the towel off me and drying my back. 'Now every Nazi Jew-killer can spot you a mile off.'

'He was religious,' I say.

You have to stand up for your grandfather even if he did accidently put your life at risk.

'Religious,' says Genia scornfully. 'That's not my idea of religious.'

For a moment I wonder if she prays to Richmal Crompton too. But I don't say anything about that because there's something even more important I need to ask her.

'If you hate Jewish people so much,' I say, 'why didn't you hand me over to the Nazis?'

'And me?' says Zelda.

I wait anxiously for Genia's answer. It's a risky question to ask a person you hope is going to look after you and protect you and give you more turnips.

Genia chews her lip and rubs her head like some people do when a question is difficult. Szymon Glick used to do it in class all the time.

'You're right,' says Genia. 'I don't like Jews. I never have. It's how I was brought up.'

My insides sink.

Zelda is glaring. I can see she's trying to think of an insult to say back at Genia.

'But,' says Genia, 'there are people I dislike much more than Jews.'

'Nazis?' I say.

'Oh yes,' says Genia. 'I hate Nazis a lot.'

I remind myself to make sure that Genia never sees Zelda's locket, which I've hidden in my boot.

'But most of all,' continues Genia, 'I hate anyone who hurts children.'

Now, with her eyes fierce, she looks even more like Mum. Even with her short hair that's sticking up from where she was rubbing it.

'When I heard a rumour the Nazis had killed the Jewish orphans,' says Genia, 'I prayed it wasn't true. That's why I was in the forest, seeing for myself.'

She screws up her face at the memory and smacks the bathwater, splashing me and Zelda.

Leopold gives a yelp and jumps back.

'Those kids have lived in this district all their lives,' says Genia. 'What sort of monsters would do that to them?'

I'm not sure if she wants an answer, so I stand quietly while she dries me and Zelda again.

Genia stops frowning and looks at us both.

'How did you manage it?' she asks. 'How did you escape from the shooting?'

I can see she does want an answer to this. But I'm not sure what to say. She thinks we're local orphans and we're not. If I tell her the truth, will she still want to look after us?

'We didn't escape from the shooting, we escaped from the train,' Zelda says to her. 'Don't you know anything?'

Genia stares at us in surprise.

I wait for her to ask us to leave.

She doesn't.

'A train from the city,' I say quietly. 'On its way to a death camp.'

Genia puts her hand on my face, just for a moment, and I can tell from her expression that it's going to be all right.

Zelda is frowning.

'If you're going to be our new mummy,' she says to Genia, 'you have to like Jewish people.'

Genia nods slowly, puffing out her cheeks as if it's a very difficult thing to think about.

'Felix can't help it,' says Zelda, pointing towards my private part.

Genia gives a long sigh.

'Neither of you can,' she says. 'Come on, kneel down so I can do your hair.'

We both kneel down with our heads over the metal bathtub.

'Keep your eyes closed,' says Genia.

She wets our hair and rubs something onto it that smells horrible. And hurts.

'Ow,' says Zelda. 'That shampoo stings.'

'It's not shampoo,' says Genia. 'It's bleach.'

I don't know what bleach is, but when I finally open my eyes I see what it does.

Zelda's hair isn't black any more, it's yellow. And Zelda is staring at me with an amazed expression, so my hair must have turned yellow too.

I know why Genia has done this.

'It's so we blend in with the straw, isn't it?' I say to her. 'For when we hide in the barn.'

Genia smiles.

'Good thought, Felix,' she says. 'But you won't be hiding in the barn any more.'

I stare at her. I don't like the sound of this. Has she decided it's too risky to have us that close to the house?

'Where will we be hiding?' I ask anxiously. 'In a haystack?'

'Out in the open,' says Genia.

I stare at her even harder.

How can we hide out in the open?

'Are you good at stories, Felix?' asks Genia.

'Yes, he is,' says Zelda. 'He's very good. Specially funny ones and sad ones.'

'Excellent,' says Genia. 'Because from now on you both have to tell people a story about yourselves. How you're two Catholic children from Pilica. How your parents were killed. How you've come to stay with your aunty, who from now on is me.'

I try to take this in.

Zelda is thinking about it too.

I'm not sure how I feel about this.

'Wouldn't the barn be safer?' I say.

Suddenly the barn doesn't seem so bad. We could play with the pig. And the chickens. I try not to think about Nazi bayonets.

'Only Jews hide in barns,' says Genia. 'And from now on you're not Jews.'

For a moment I think Zelda is going to argue, but she doesn't.

I don't either, but I'm still not sure.

'Which would you prefer?' says Genia. 'Being stuck in a barn the whole time, or being able to run around and play outdoors and sleep in a bed?'

'A bed,' I say.

'A bed,' says Zelda.

It's a good point. We haven't slept in a real bed for ages.

I'm starting to see that hiding in the open could be better, except for one problem. I look down at my private part.

Genia sees me looking and nods her head.

'That is the weak link in our plan,' she says.

I wish it wasn't. But I do have one hopeful thought.

'When I was younger,' I tell Genia, 'my parents hid me in a Catholic orphanage. I told the other boys I'd been circumcised for medical reasons because I'd had an illness of the private part.'

Genia shakes her head.

'Good story,' she says. 'But the Nazis have heard it a million times before.'

We all look at my private part.

'Only one thing to do,' says Genia.

'What?' I say, hoping it won't be painful.

'Don't show it to anybody,' says Genia.

I nod. I'll have to hope no Nazis want to see it.

'I'll make sure he doesn't show it to anybody,' says Zelda.

'Good girl,' says Genia. 'Now, we have to find new names for you.'

Zelda's eyes light up.

'William and Violet Elizabeth,' she says.

Genia thinks about this.

'They're names from our favourite stories,' I explain. 'Our favourite story-writer Richmal Crompton is English. When her stories are changed into Polish, the names stay English.'

'English names aren't a good idea,' says Genia. 'The Nazis are at war with England.'

'We like those names,' says Zelda fiercely.

Genia rolls her eyes.

'All right,' she says. 'But we have to make them Polish. Wilhelm and Violetta.'

Zelda grins.

I'm happy too. Now it's almost like Richmal Crompton will be helping Genia look after us.

This bed is comfortable and warm, and Genia doesn't snore that much, and she's left a lamp burning low so we won't be scared.

But I just can't get to sleep.

Neither can Zelda.

'Felix,' she says, nudging me in the ribs. 'Tell me a William and Violet Elizabeth story.'

'You mean Wilhelm and Violetta,' I whisper. 'And don't fidget. You'll pull the covers off Genia and wake her up.'

It's very kind of Genia to let us share her bed. Luckily there's space because her husband's away.

Zelda lies very still and I whisper a story to her. It's about how Wilhelm and Violetta are rescued by a kind lady called Genia. They live happily ever after with Genia, and with her friendly dog who likes to be tickled, and with a nice pig who likes to be tickled too, and with some very loyal chickens. Sometimes Wilhelm and Violetta play hide-and-seek with the chickens, and at no stage do the chickens betray them to the Nazis.

By the time I've finished the story, Zelda is asleep.

'Good story,' whispers Genia.

I'm startled. I hadn't realised she was listening.

'Can you tell another one?' she says. 'About a Polish man who's forced to go to Germany to work for the Nazis and who comes home safely.'

I look at her, confused. I'm not sure if I know enough to tell a story like that.

'He likes to be tickled,' says Genia.

While I'm waiting for my imagination to come up with something, I see the sad smile on her face and I realise who she's talking about.

'Does he come home at weekends?' I ask. 'Your husband.'

Genia shakes her head.

'I haven't seen him for two years,' she says quietly.

'That's terrible,' I say.

I tell Genia the story she asked for, but while I'm telling it I'm also thinking about something else.

Why do people start wars when they know so many sad things are going to happen?

I don't get it.

After I finish the story, me and Genia talk for a while. She doesn't get it either.

Finally she says, 'I must let you sleep. Good night, Wilhelm. And thank you.'

'Thank you,' I say. 'For protecting me and Zelda. I mean me and Violetta.'

We're both lying here, breathing quietly, Zelda asleep between us.

I don't know Genia very well, but I can guess what she's thinking.

The same as me.

We're both hoping our stories come true.

Then me and Zelda lived happily with Genia for more than a week without any sad things happening.

We also lived happily with Leopold the dog and Trotski the pig.

And a bit less happily with the chickens, who won't stay still long enough for us to feed them with our automatic chicken-feeding machine.

'Stop running away,' says Zelda crossly, waving her arms at them and chasing them all over the barn. 'You have to line up.'

I'm not surprised the chickens are a bit scared. They've probably never seen a gherkin tin nailed to a rafter before. Specially not one with a string hanging down that you have to pull with your beak to make the tin wobble and the grains of wheat fall through the holes in the bottom.

New inventions are always a bit confusing and scary. I remember how nervous Mum and Dad were at home when we first got a tin-opener. You can't blame these chickens for feeling the same.

'Give them time to get used to it,' I say to Zelda.

But Zelda grabs a chicken and staggers with it over to the chicken-feeding machine. She holds its beak and tries to make it pull the string. The chicken spits the string out, squawks indignantly and flaps out of her arms.

'Idiot,' Zelda yells at it. 'You have to pull the string. Don't you know anything?'

I smile to myself.

When Zelda asked me to build the automatic 1965 chicken-feeding machine from our story, I had a feeling it might be a bit too advanced for these 1942 chickens. But I didn't care because it was such fun inventing and making it. Nothing takes your mind off sad war things like an automatic chicken-feeding machine.

For a while, anyway.

'You're all idiots,' Zelda is yelling at the chickens. 'And Nazis.'

Leopold the dog and Trotski the pig are cowering in the corner of the barn.

The chickens are looking pretty stressed too, which I'm now remembering isn't a good thing.

Before Genia went into town this morning, she explained that these days eggs are so precious they're like money. In fact, eggs are Genia's only money. Which is why instead of us eating them, she takes them to town to swap for things.

When she gets home this afternoon I don't want her to find all the chickens have stopped laying eggs because Zelda has been calling them Nazis.

I decide to give the chickens a break.

'Let's play hide-and-seek,' I say to Zelda.

She looks at me like I'm an inventor who's not taking inventing seriously enough. But after a few moments she grins.

'All right,' she says.

We help Leopold hide in his kennel and we give Trotski a hand to lie down behind an old horse harness. After that we burrow down into the straw.

'Come and find us,' Zelda calls to the chickens as she snuggles next to me.

I'm not sure if the chickens will be any better at this than they are at feeding themselves automatically, but it doesn't matter. It's fun here in the straw with no Nazis around.

'Felix,' whispers Zelda. 'I like it here. Can we stay here for ever?'

At first I think she means in the straw, which would get a bit itchy after a while because of the insects.

'On this farm,' says Zelda.

'I hope so,' I reply, but before I can explain that it's up to Genia, the barn door gives a loud creak.

I blow the dust off my glasses and peer out through the straw.

The barn door was shut to keep the chickens in,

but not locked. Now somebody, I can't see who, is slowly pulling it open.

'Shhh,' I whisper to Zelda.

We hold our breaths.

Leopold barks.

I pray it's just Genia home early and I wait for her to step inside.

She doesn't.

Instead, a lump of something is tossed through the doorway and lands with a splat on the dirt floor.

A lump of raw meat.

I stare at it.

This is incredible. Meat is even more precious than eggs. Who would throw a lump of meat onto the ground?

'Good boy,' I hear a voice whispering from outside. 'Good boy, Leopold.'

Leopold comes panting out of his kennel and goes straight to the meat and starts eating it.

I can't believe what I'm seeing. Leopold is an important family member and we love him a lot, but you don't give meat to a dog, not in wartime, not when people are lucky if they have it once a month.

I'm tempted to crawl out of the straw to remind Genia about this, but before I can, somebody comes into the barn and it's not Genia.

It's a kid.

He's about my age with dark hair and old grown-up clothes that are too big for him. He kneels down next to Leopold, who's still scoffing the meat.

'Good boy,' he says in a gruff voice, and gives Leopold a hug.

Gently I squeeze Zelda's arm to let her know we should stay hidden until I can work out who this kid is. We can't be too careful. Kids like rewards too, even if they don't drink vodka.

Zelda is stiff with fright. I know what she's hoping. That the chickens don't suddenly get good at hide-and-seek and find us.

Wait a minute, that kid looks a bit familiar.

Have I met him before?

While I'm trying to think if I have, Trotski the pig goes over to the meat and starts gobbling it too.

Leopold doesn't mind, but the kid does.

'Get lost,' he says, and smacks Trotski on the head.

Before I can stop her, Zelda is on her feet, straw flying everywhere, striding towards the kid.

I stand up too.

The kid jumps back, startled, dark eyes glaring.

'Don't hit Trotski,' Zelda yells at the kid. 'He doesn't like being hit. He only likes being tickled.'

Zelda puts her arms round Trotski, who looks slightly dazed by all the attention.

The kid grabs Zelda and gets one arm round her neck. In his other hand he suddenly has a knife close to her throat.

There's blood on the knife.

Please, I beg silently, let it be blood from the meat.

57

'Stop being a bully,' squeals Zelda.

I take a step towards them. The kid moves the knife even closer to Zelda's throat.

'Let her go,' I say. 'We're Leopold's friends too.'

The kid doesn't reply. Just glowers at me with the angriest eyes I've ever seen.

'Leopold isn't your friend,' Zelda says to the kid. 'Bite him, Leopold.'

Leopold growls, but stays with the meat. I don't think he likes fighting.

I'm going to have to grab the knife. I don't like fighting either and I haven't really done much, but I can't think of any other way.

The kid looks like he's done a lot of fighting. He's got a big scab on his forehead.

Here goes.

But before I can fling myself at him, the kid suddenly mutters some swear words and pushes Zelda away and runs out of the barn.

I let him go.

'Are you all right?' I ask Zelda, helping her up and checking her for stab wounds.

'Children shouldn't play with real knives,' she says tearfully. 'Doesn't he know anything?'

I hug her. Leopold licks her. Trotski burps in a sympathetic way. The chickens run around clucking excitedly, but I think that's just because they've found us.

We creep to the barn door, but there's no sign of the kid.

'Let's chase after him,' mutters Zelda. 'With sticks.'

But we don't. We're not the sort of people who go looking for trouble, not even when we're angry.

I hope we never see that kid again.

After a while Genia arrives home from town.

She's got things she bought with the eggs. Trousers for me and a dress and shoes for Zelda and warm underwear for us both.

In the kitchen, while we try them on, we tell Genia about the horrible kid. She examines the last bit of the meat we've saved as evidence.

'Rabbit,' she says. 'I could have made a stew with that.'

'Or a pet,' says Zelda.

Genia frowns, thinking.

'That boy must have escaped,' she says.

'Escaped from where?' I say.

'The orphanage,' says Genia. 'Apart from you two, the only other kids who ever made friends with Leopold were the orphans. The ones the Nazis murdered.'

I look at Genia, surprised.

She used to hate Jewish people. Why did she let them be friends with her dog?

'The Nazis made the orphans do farm work,' says Genia. 'Growing food for the German army. The kids helped me plant my fields earlier this year.

They did a good job. Beautiful crop of cabbages I had, before the Nazis took them.'

Zelda is frowning now.

'If the Jewish orphans were good at Nazi cabbages,' she says to Genia, 'why didn't the Nazis let them keep being alive?'

Genia scowls.

'Who knows why those slugs do anything,' she says. 'I heard a rumour they needed the orphanage building for something else.'

I'm shocked. Killing innocent children just to get their bedrooms.

I'm also shocked to hear that the kid with the knife is Jewish. A Jewish orphan whose friends are all dead except for Leopold.

I wish I'd known that.

Perhaps me and Zelda and the chickens could have been a bit friendlier.

Then Genia helped me and Zelda to be Wilhelm and Violetta. She got us fake Wilhelm and Violetta identity cards from a priest in exchange for eggs. She told us all about the place where Wilhelm and Violetta were born. For two weeks she tested us on our Wilhelm and Violetta childhoods.

'What did your father do?'

'He had a shop selling lamp oil,' I say.

'What was your mother's first name?'

'Jadwiga,' says Zelda.

'What street was your school in?'

'Poznod Street,' I say. 'Next to the bank.'

'What pets did you have?'

'A chicken called Goebbels,' says Zelda.

'No,' says Genia. 'Not Goebbels. That was your pet chicken when you were Zelda. Now that you're Violetta, your pet chicken was called Kranki, remember?'

Poor Zelda. Genia is a tough questioner. I think

she could be a Nazi herself if she wanted to be. Luckily she doesn't.

'Remember?' she says to Zelda again.

'Yes,' sighs Zelda.

I hope Zelda can remember. Specially this morning, because we're on our way into town for the first time. So far, as we walk along the road past the local farms, we haven't met anybody. But I can see somebody coming in the distance.

Suddenly I don't feel ready.

'Genia,' I say. 'Can we go home and practise some more?'

'No,' says Genia. 'People want to meet you. They've seen me buying things for you and they're getting suspicious. We can't put it off any longer.'

Yes we can, I want to say. But how can you argue with someone as kind and generous and caring as Genia? Look what she's doing for us, and she doesn't even like Jewish people that much.

'Kranki,' Zelda is repeating sternly to herself as she clomps along the road in her new shoes. 'Kranki.'

The person coming towards us is a big woman with a grey headscarf and a red face.

I'm shivering with nerves now, even though the sun is shining and my hair is gleaming yellow because Genia put more bleach on it this morning.

'You'll be fine,' Genia whispers to me and Zelda. 'Just don't drop those eggs.'

We're carrying eggs in boxes. They're packed in

straw, but mine are wobbling around because I'm trembling so much.

'Good morning, Mrs Placzek,' says Genia in the same fake friendly voice she used with the Nazi soldiers.

'Good morning,' says the scarf woman. She smiles at Genia for about one second, turns, and looks at me and Zelda.

Suddenly I know what an egg feels like. My disguise feels about as strong as a very thin shell.

'These are the children I was telling you about,' says Genia. 'Wilhelm and Violetta.'

Mrs Placzek clucks sympathetically.

'Poor orphans,' she says, reaching out.

For a moment I think she's going to touch my hair to see if the yellow comes off, but she doesn't. Instead she grabs my cheek and gives it a squeeze.

'Your poor dead mummy and daddy,' she says.

'Jadwiga,' says Zelda.

'My father had a shop selling lamp oil,' I say.

Genia is looking a bit concerned. I think it's because we're answering Mrs Placzek's questions even before she's asked them.

'What have you got there?' says Mrs Placzek, pointing to my egg box.

I can't think what to say. We haven't practised this one. But after a moment my brain clears.

'Eggs,' I say.

'Lucky boy,' says Mrs Placzek. 'I love eggs. Delicious.'

Once again I'm not sure what to say. I haven't eaten an egg since I was little. I can't even remember what they taste like.

'Eggs are good for us,' says Zelda to Mrs Placzek. 'Goebbels told me.'

Mrs Placzek frowns.

Zelda's eyes go wide as she realises what she's just said.

'I mean Kranki,' she blurts out.

Genia is frowning too now.

Mrs Placzek laughs.

'Children,' she says to Genia. 'What imaginations. It must be a joy having them around.'

'It is,' says Genia, smiling, but still sort of frowning at the same time.

I don't care. Mrs Placzek hasn't run off to fetch the Nazis. She's smiling and waving to us now as we say goodbye and walk away.

Our disguises are working.

A horse and cart is approaching, but I'm feeling much more confident. I stay feeling more confident until I recognise the old man driving the cart.

It's the turnip man.

Zelda recognises him too, I can tell from the little squeak she gives.

As the cart gets closer, I see the reward notice still stuck to the side. The cart doesn't have any turnips in it today, probably so he can fit more Jews in.

'It's OK,' I whisper to Zelda. 'He won't recognise us.'

I hope I'm right.

'Good morning, Mr Krol,' says Genia.

Mr Krol doesn't stop the cart. His only reply is a grunt. But as he rumbles past, he stares at me and Zelda for a long time, not smiling.

I feel a desperate urge to tell him my father had a shop selling lamp oil.

I manage not to.

'Bad-tempered old turnip,' mutters Genia once he's gone.

I agree, but at least he didn't try to get us into his cart. Our disguises are working even with somebody we've met before.

I think we're going to be OK.

After a couple of minutes I glance over my shoulder. I can still see the cart in the distance. Mr Krol is turned round in his seat, still staring at us.

It's all right, I tell myself. He's probably just thirsty for a drink of vodka and he's wishing me and Zelda were Jews.

Then we got to the town and it wasn't all right.

At first I felt at home. The stone houses and slate roofs and cobbled streets were a bit like the ones in the town where I lived when I was little. When I was Felix, not Wilhelm.

But in the town square there's something I've never seen before.

Big wooden posts with dead people hanging from them.

'Don't look,' says Genia to me and Zelda. She tries to hurry us across the square.

But we are looking. You have to. It's terrible. The hanging people with ropes round their necks aren't soldiers, they're just people. A lady in a green dress. An older lady wearing an apron. Several men in shirts. One in pyjamas.

The other people in the square aren't looking. They're hurrying past, staring at the cobbles. Which is what Genia is trying to make us do.

'Are those people dead?' says Zelda, pointing. She's starting to get upset.

'Yes,' whispers Genia. 'They were sheltering the Jew in the green dress. The Nazis caught them and killed them and everyone else in their family.'

That's awful. And it's extra awful just to leave them there like that.

The Nazis must be doing it as a warning.

To people like us.

'I hate Nazis,' says Zelda bitterly.

Genia gives her an anxious look as we cross the square.

I see why. A group of Nazi soldiers are strolling towards us. A couple of them are looking at us.

'Come on, Wilhelm and Violetta,' says Genia loudly. 'Be careful with those eggs.'

I'm finding it hard to be careful with the eggs. I'm having too many feelings all at once. That could be me and Zelda and Genia hanging there. And if it was, Genia would be dead for looking after me, and Zelda would be dead for being my friend, and it would all be my fault.

Genia takes us to a shop on the other side of the square.

On the door is a sign.

NO DOGS OR JEWS.

I hesitate.

'Don't dawdle, Wilhelm,' says Genia. 'You're blocking the doorway.'

I go in, trying to look like I couldn't care less about the sign.

'That sign isn't fair,' says Zelda loudly. 'Our dog Leopold would have hurt feelings if he saw that sign.'

Behind the counter is a big woman with her sleeves rolled up. She does the sort of laugh people do when they're not really amused.

'My dog already got hurt feelings,' she says. 'Right around the time I decided not to waste any more food on it.'

Zelda stares at the woman, shocked.

'Wilhelm and Violetta,' says Genia hastily, 'this is Mrs Szynsky.'

'Hello,' I say politely.

'Hello,' mutters Zelda.

Mrs Szynsky doesn't reply. She just looks me and Zelda up and down.

'Must have a lot of food to spare,' she says to Genia. 'Oh well, your loss.'

She fiddles with her blonde hair for a while, then points to our egg boxes as if she's only just noticed them.

'How many eggs?' she says.

'Fourteen,' says Genia.

We all put our boxes on the counter and Mrs Szynsky counts the eggs, picking each one up and peering at it closely.

'What do you want?' she says, not looking at Genia.

'A coat and a hat for each of the kids,' says Genia. 'When they were bombed out in Pilica they lost all their winter clothes.'

Mrs Szynsky looks scornful.

'For fourteen eggs?' she says. 'Not a chance. You can forget the hats for a start.'

'Ten eggs for the coats,' says Genia. 'With scarves.'

While Genia and Mrs Szynsky haggle, I peer around the shop. It's full of amazing things. Furniture and piles of clothes and unusual shoes and stuffed animals and paintings and decorated plates and glass cases full of jewellery.

Genia is holding Zelda's hand, but not mine.

I wander around the shop, gazing at everything.

Up the back, next to a pile of clocks, I find a polished wooden box.

Inside are the shiniest knives and forks and spoons I've ever seen. Even shinier than the ones we used to have when I was little.

I take out one of the spoons.

I wish I could buy it for Genia. She's only got wooden ones.

'Put it back,' hisses a voice.

Guiltily I put the spoon back.

A boy of about my age leaps out from behind a rack of hanging suits and snatches the box.

'No touching the goods,' he says in a bossy voice.

That doesn't seem fair. Next to us two burly

farmers are trying on shiny red waistcoats. I open my mouth to point out that they're touching the goods. But I remember I'm Wilhelm, not Felix, and close it again.

'This is my family's shop,' says the boy. 'You were going to steal that spoon, weren't you?'

He's glaring at me, his lips wet and his face pink. His hair is so fair I can even see the pink skin on his head.

'No,' I say. 'I wasn't. Honest.'

I can feel my face going pink too, with panic. If he calls the police . . .

The boy gives me a wet grin.

'Only kidding,' he says.

I stare at him, stunned.

'Can't you take a joke?' he says, looking a bit offended.

I pull myself together.

'Course I can,' I say, dizzy with relief. I hold out my hand. 'I'm Wilhelm Nowak.'

I shake the boy's cold damp hand.

'I'm Cyryl,' he says.

Suddenly he leans towards me like I'm his best friend.

'Hey,' he says, tapping the cutlery box. 'Guess how much this cost.'

I haven't got a clue. Thousands of zloty probably. Millions.

'Two eggs,' says Cyryl.

I wait for him to tell me he's only kidding again.

'From the dumb Jews,' he says, grinning. 'My dad takes eggs and milk and bread over to that other part of town, you know, where we put all the Jews, what's it called . . .?'

'I don't know,' I say.

I do, it's called a ghetto. But I don't tell Cyryl that. If he doesn't know, Wilhelm shouldn't.

'Anyway,' says Cyryl, pointing around the shop, 'the dumb Jews swapped all this stuff for bits of food.'

'Perhaps they were hungry,' I murmur, and immediately wish I hadn't.

But Cyryl hasn't noticed. He's grinning at me and licking his lips. His teeth are crooked and he's got a dribble problem.

'What's the difference between a Jew and a rat?' he says.

'Don't know,' I say, trying to be Wilhelm.

'Once you've got them out from under your floorboards,' says Cyryl, 'who cares?'

I can feel my face going pink again. With anger this time.

Don't do anything silly, I beg myself. Like opening the cutlery box. And doing something to Cyryl with a fork.

'Hey,' says Cyryl, stepping close to me again like he's sharing another big secret. 'When Jews say their prayers, it makes cheese go mouldy. My dad told me.'

I struggle to be Wilhelm.

Cyryl looks at me for a moment.

'You're new,' he says. 'I haven't seen you before.'

'We just moved here,' I say. 'From Pilica.'

'If you want,' says Cyryl, 'you can join my gang.'

I don't know what to say. I wouldn't join Cyryl's gang if you gave me a whole box of cutlery and an uncircumcised private part.

I'm saved by a yelling voice.

'Cyryl, come back here, you haven't finished this job.'

A teenage girl with blonde pigtails is sticking her head out of a back room and glaring at Cyryl.

His shoulders slump and he gives her a sulky look.

'Sisters,' he says to me, scowling. 'They're worse than Jews.'

I nod. I don't trust myself to actually say anything. Cyryl doesn't notice. He's too busy being indignant.

'I do everything around here,' he says. 'I have to sort through all the new stuff that comes in. Half of it's junk. The Jews are always trying to cheat us.'

'Cyryl,' yells his sister, furious.

'That's all Jew junk there,' says Cyryl, pointing to a big wooden crate as he walks off.

I wait till Cyryl's in the back room before I look in the crate. Perhaps there'll be something cheap in there that Genia needs. She might be able to add it to the coats for the same number of eggs.

The stuff in the crate doesn't look like junk to me. There are cooking pots, shoes, ornaments, all sorts of things. A bit scuffed but not bad. There's even a book. OK, it looks like it's been in a fire, some of the pages are a bit burned and . . .

I pick it up and glance at the cover.

My heart jolts.

It's a Richmal Crompton book. In Polish, just like the ones I used to have, except this is one I've never read.

I try to be Wilhelm and drop it back into the crate, but I can't help it, I'm Felix and I stuff it inside my shirt.

Cyryl said this was all junk so I'm not really stealing.

Yes I am, but I don't care.

Suddenly I do care.

A voice is screaming at me. A voice so angry I can't even make out the words.

Is it Cyryl? His sister? Mrs Szynsky?

I turn, weak with fear.

And go even weaker.

It isn't any of the Szynsky family, it's a Nazi soldier.

He's got a rifle and he's pointing it at my head.

Then the Nazi soldier started waving his rifle. I still didn't understand any of the Nazi words he was yelling, but I could see he was ordering me out of the shop.

I felt sick.

What's the Nazi punishment for stealing a Richmal Crompton book? Getting hanged from a big wooden post in the town square with the other dead people?

I walk slowly towards the door of the shop.

Once I'm outside I'll run. It's all I can do. The book is inside my shirt, so I can't pretend I was buying it.

I don't look at Genia and Zelda. If I ignore them, maybe the Nazi soldier will too.

But Genia doesn't ignore me. She grabs my hand.

'Don't,' I whisper. 'The Nazi soldier will think you're in on it.'

Genia gives me a puzzled look. She doesn't let go of my hand.

'Come on, Wilhelm and Violetta,' she says. 'The soldier is ordering everybody outside to watch the Hitler Youth parade.'

She drags me and Zelda towards the door.

Everybody else in the shop is leaving too. Customers, Mrs Szynsky, shop assistants, Cyryl and his big sister.

Outside, hundreds of people are standing around the edges of the town square. We join them.

At first I'm not sure what's going on. I'm just dizzy with relief at not getting arrested.

'I can't see any parade,' says Zelda loudly.

'Shhh,' says Genia.

I realise why Genia wants Zelda to behave herself. Nazi soldiers are strutting about, bossing people and making everyone stand neatly.

Faintly, in the distance, I can hear the sound of marching boots.

Everybody is looking towards the far end of the square. The sound gets louder. A column of Nazis appears, marching in rows of four into the square.

There's something strange about them.

Compared to the other Nazi soldiers, they look a bit small.

As they get closer, I see why. They're boys about my age, maybe a couple of years older. All wearing Nazi uniforms and gleaming Nazi boots. They don't have guns, which is a good thing. Most of them have really sneering expressions. They don't look like the sort of people who would handle guns responsibly.

Genia jabs me with her elbow.

'Lower your eyes,' she hisses.

I see that all around the square, people are taking off their hats and looking at the ground.

I bow my head. But I keep watching from under my eyebrows as the marching boys get closer.

I've heard about the Hitler Youth. Adolf Hitler, the leader of the Nazis, started the Hitler Youth for German kids who are too young to join the army but want to strut around full of themselves anyway.

I've heard they can be very violent, even without guns.

'What fine young men,' says Mrs Szynsky, who's standing next to us. 'You could join them, Cyryl, if you weren't such a slob.'

'They're German,' says Cyryl. 'I'm not German.'

'You're still a slob,' says his sister.

I stop listening to Cyryl and his sister bickering because a thought hits me.

'Genia,' I whisper, my head still bowed. 'Is that why the Nazis wanted the Jewish orphans' bedrooms? For the Hitler Youth?'

I look sideways at her.

She nods.

The Hitler Youth have almost reached us now and everybody is bowing their heads even lower.

Except Zelda, who is glaring at the Hitler Youth and poking her tongue out.

'Don't,' I hiss at her in panic.

Genia sees what Zelda is doing.

She grabs Zelda and tries to hide her by standing in front of her.

But it's too late.

Cyryl also sees what Zelda is doing, and he starts giggling loudly.

One of the Hitler Youth at the front of the marching column yells something to the others and they all stop.

Right next to us.

Four of the Hitler Youth step out of the column and stride towards us. Behind them, a Nazi soldier raises his gun like he's keen to join in.

My insides are throbbing with fear.

I get ready to throw myself at the Hitler Youth if they touch Zelda.

But it isn't Zelda they touch. It's Cyryl. They grab him and slap him and punch him really hard. His mother lets out a shriek, but when they turn to her she smothers her mouth with her hand.

They punch and slap Cyryl some more.

I get furious.

I can't help it. When I see how much those Hitler Youth thugs are enjoying what they're doing, I stop being Wilhelm and take a step towards them.

As soon as I do, I come to my senses. What am I doing? I'm not a fighter. I can't protect Cyryl. All I'm doing is getting my family into trouble.

Genia grabs me and pulls me back.

The jolt makes the Richmal Crompton book fall out of my shirt onto the ground. For a moment I think I'm sprung. I brace myself to be arrested.

But nobody notices.

Mrs Szynsky is too busy helping Cyryl to his feet. The Hitler Youth thugs are too busy taking their places back in the column.

I crouch down to grab the book.

Just before my hand makes contact with it, the Hitler Youth leader yells something again.

I look up. He's not yelling at me, he's yelling at the column to start marching again, which they do.

But as the column marches off, one of the other Hitler Youth, not one of the thugs, stares at the book on the ground in front of me.

And does an amazing thing.

He grins at me. And with a small movement of his hand, so the other Hitler Youth can't see him, he gives me a thumbs up.

I blink. Did he really do that?

Is he telling me he's a Richmal Crompton fan too?

I grab the book and stuff it back inside my shirt and stand up and try to look like nothing has happened.

Nobody seems to be looking at me.

Well, hardly anybody.

The Hitler Youth column is halfway across the square now, but the boy who saw the book is still throwing glances back in my direction.

Somebody else is looking at me too.

Cyryl.

His mum is trying to wipe away the blood that's trickling out of his nose. He keeps moving his head. He wants her to leave him alone so he can do something else.

Stare at me and Zelda with total hatred.

I look away, but my insides stay knotted with worry. This is the last thing me and Zelda need.

An enemy with a gang.

Then me and Zelda and Genia went home. We didn't say much on the walk back. Genia didn't lose her temper till we were in the house.

'That was very foolish,' she yells.

At first I think she's angry with me for stealing the Richmal Crompton book. Except I don't think she saw it when I dropped it in the town square and it's been hidden in my shirt ever since.

'Very foolish and very naughty,' yells Genia.

I realise it's Zelda she's telling off.

'Poking your tongue out at Nazis,' yells Genia. 'What were you thinking, Violetta?'

'She's only six,' I say.

I agree Zelda was foolish, but I can see she's scared at how cross Genia is, and sometimes you have to look after your family even when they have been naughty.

'You're old enough to understand what Nazis are like,' Genia says to Zelda. 'You saw what they did to the poor Jewish orphans. And the orphans weren't even rude to them.'

'If they try to take our bedroom,' says Zelda. 'I'll be very rude to them.'

She isn't looking scared any more.

Genia sighs.

'I hate Nazis,' says Zelda.

I want to explain to Genia that this isn't the way to protect Zelda. That giving angry examples of how bad the Nazis are isn't going to make Zelda behave herself in public. It'll only make her worse.

Suddenly I know what I have to do. On the way home I was trying to decide, but now I know it's for the best.

So Genia understands.

So we can help Zelda.

I go into the bedroom. Next to the wall in the corner is a crack between two floorboards. I squeeze my fingers in and pull Zelda's locket out of its hiding place.

I take a deep breath.

This is risky, but sometimes you have to take a risk to protect your family.

I go back into the kitchen.

'Genia,' I say. 'You know how you said I couldn't help being Jewish?'

Genia nods.

I can see she's wondering what I'm on about.

'Well,' I say, 'here's something Zelda can't help.'

I show Genia the locket.

Zelda is staring. She thought she'd lost her locket in the barn. I'm pretty sure she didn't ever want to see it again.

Genia is staring too, at the tiny photo inside the locket. The photo of a Nazi dad in uniform and a Nazi mum gazing at him adoringly.

'Zelda's parents,' I say.

I want Genia to understand. To see why Zelda has bad feelings about Nazis, apart from them being vicious thugs and killers. To understand that some of her bad feelings are about her mum and dad.

Genia looks at the photo for a long time.

She gives a big sigh and looks at me.

'Why didn't you tell me?' she says.

'You hate Nazis,' I say. 'I didn't want you to hate Zelda.'

Genia sighs again. She puts one arm round Zelda and the other round me.

'Neither of you can help who your parents are,' she says quietly. 'Do you understand that, Zelda? Your mummy and daddy aren't your fault.'

Zelda pulls away from Genia.

'They aren't my mummy and daddy,' she says crossly. 'I'm Violetta. Don't you know anything?'

I wait for Genia to get angry again, but she doesn't, she just nods.

'Good girl,' she says, putting both arms round Zelda. 'You're learning.'

They look so content, hugging like that.

I don't like to interrupt.

But I have to.

'Genia,' I say. 'About Zelda's real parents. There's another problem.'

Genia looks at me over the top of Zelda's head. She leans across and ruffles my hair and puts her finger to her lips.

'Zelda's trying to forget about her parents,' she says. 'We have to help her do that.'

I sigh.

Genia doesn't understand.

Kids like us don't forget our real parents.

Not ever.

And until Zelda feels better about hers, she's going to keep poking her tongue out at Nazis.

Then I helped Zelda have happy memories of her real parents so she wouldn't be so cross and upset about them being Nazis.

Leopold helped too.

Well, we tried.

'Zelda,' I say as we sit in front of the wood stove. 'Give Leopold a hug. See if it brings back any happy memories.'

Zelda looks at me as if I've got leaf-mould madness. But she does it anyway because hugging Leopold is one of her favourite things to do.

Leopold likes it too. His tail is whacking the kitchen floor just at the thought.

Zelda puts her arms round him and buries her face in his neck fur.

'I love you, Leopold,' she says, her voice muffled.

'Any happy memories?' I say softly after a while.

Zelda keeps her face buried, thinking.

'Yes,' she says. 'I can remember when I hugged Leopold this morning before breakfast.'

I try to think of something that will help her have earlier happy memories.

'Your daddy had whiskers like Leopold,' I say.

Leopold looks a bit offended.

'No he didn't,' says Zelda, still muffled. 'My daddy's whiskers were short. And he didn't lick my ear.'

Leopold stops licking Zelda's ear and gives me an apologetic look.

'It's all right,' I say to him. 'You're doing a good job helping Zelda.'

I give Leopold a pat and he gives me a loving look and suddenly, gazing into his gentle eyes, I'm having memories of my own.

Dad giving me a bath and drying me on our kitchen table.

Mum blowing raspberries on my tummy.

'You're helping me too,' I whisper to Leopold.

I try to feel happy but it's not easy.

Zelda looks up, concerned, and watches me for a moment.

'See?' she says. 'Memories aren't happy, they're sad. Don't you know anything?'

Every day it's the same.

I do my best, but Zelda is a very stubborn person.

Like today. We're doing drawing in the barn.

Or rather, I'm letting Zelda do most of the drawing because there's only one pencil.

Earlier, when it was my go of the pencil, I did a diagram of how the automatic chicken-feeding machine works.

Now I'm nailing the diagram to the wall under the gherkin tin so the chickens can see what they have to do.

Leopold and Trotski are staring at me. They're looking a bit disappointed, possibly because there aren't any dogs or pigs in the diagram.

I give them both a tickle.

'Don't worry,' I say to them. 'Me and Violetta will invent automatic feeding machines for you next.'

Animals get very anxious in wartime. If the humans get killed, who's going to feed them?

I go over to Zelda to see how her drawing's going.

'That lady's got a very pretty hat,' I say, pointing to the person Zelda has drawn. 'Who is it?'

'It's Violetta's mummy,' says Zelda. 'She wears her pretty hat when she kills Nazis.'

The paper Zelda's drawing on is old shop paper that has been wrapped round face powder or something. There's a pink stain in the middle which Zelda turns into a dead Nazi's brains leaking out.

I stare at the drawing, worry nagging inside me. If I can't find a way to help Zelda feel better about her parents, I hate to think what's going to happen next time she meets a Nazi.

'Zelda,' I say quietly. 'Why don't you do a picture of your real mummy and daddy? From when you were little. When they took you on holiday or gave you a present or did something fun with you.'

Zelda looks at me. She doesn't say anything, but I can see she doesn't like the idea much.

Leopold and Trotski come over. Leopold licks Zelda's knee. Trotski blows some snot in her direction. I can see they're both trying to help. It's their way of telling Zelda they'd like to see a nice picture of her real mummy and daddy too.

Zelda moves the pencil to another part of the paper and starts a new drawing.

'Thanks,' I whisper to them both.

While Zelda draws, I tell a story to inspire her.

It's about a friend of William and Violet Elizabeth's called Zelda. Zelda's parents accidently drown her collection of ants while they're watering the garden. Zelda is very angry, but her parents say they're sorry and cuddle her and Zelda feels better.

'And then do some other ants kill her parents?' says Zelda.

I sigh. It's not a very good story, but I'm doing my best.

'Maybe,' I say. 'But Zelda discovers that even when her parents do bad things, they still love her.'

'How can they still love her if they're dead?' says Zelda.

I sigh again. I'm getting confused now. Stories

always work best when you don't try to tell people what they're about.

I see that Zelda has drawn a happy child holding hands with two happy grown-ups.

'Is that your real mummy and daddy?' I say hopefully.

'No,' says Zelda.

Suddenly I can't stand it any more. Why can't Zelda see how important this is?

'Just draw a picture of your real mummy and daddy,' I say to her crossly.

As soon as I've said it, I feel awful. I know how sad I get thinking about my parents. And I'm ten. How sad must it be for a little kid?

Zelda is looking at me, frowning. She holds up her drawing.

'This is Wilhelm's mummy and daddy,' she says. 'They've come to cheer you up cause you're unhappy.'

I don't know what to say.

Zelda puts the drawing down and gives me a hug.

'They love you very much,' she whispers. 'They don't mind that you're Jewish.'

I hug Zelda tight. I can't believe how lucky I am to have her as my family.

'Leopold and Trotski and the chickens don't mind that you're Jewish either,' whispers Zelda.

She doesn't have to tell me that because I can tell from the way Leopold is licking my hand and

Trotski is dribbling snot onto my boots and the chickens are pecking at my bootlaces.

But it's a very kind thing to say. Zelda may be only six but she's got the kindness of a ten-year-old.

'Sorry I got cross,' I say.

'That's all right,' she says.

I take a deep breath. I mustn't give up. I must find a way. I must do everything I can to protect Zelda and her loving heart.

Suddenly I hear the distant growl of a truck engine.

Leopold barks.

I rush to the barn door and peer out across the fields.

Oh no.

'Quick,' I say to Zelda. 'Into the house.'

I grab her hand and her pencil and paper and we run across the farmyard into the kitchen.

Genia is in the bedroom having a rest. I bang on the door.

'Genia,' I yell. 'Wake up. The Nazis are back.'

Then Genia told me and Zelda to stay in the house while she went out to see what the Nazi soldiers want.

Suddenly it hits me.

The Richmal Crompton book, I bet that's what they want. Cyryl probably complained to the Nazis about me stealing the book from his family's shop and they've come to get it.

And me.

I peer through the kitchen window. It's the same two Nazi soldiers from the first day when me and Zelda were hiding in the barn.

But Genia isn't wearing any makeup or perfume this time. When I yelled about the Nazis, she jumped up from her bed and went straight outside.

Next to me Zelda is watching the Nazi soldiers through the window too. And poking her tongue out at them.

'Zelda,' I whisper frantically. 'Stop that.'

Luckily the Nazi soldiers aren't looking in our direction. They're both turned towards Genia. But they aren't grinning and sniffing her wrist this time.

They're shouting at her.

'I hate them,' mutters Zelda.

One of the soldiers grabs Genia and pulls her over to the barn. They push her inside and go in after her.

My mind is racing.

Of course. They must think I've hidden the Richmal Crompton book in the straw. When they don't find it, they'll get even angrier with Genia. And they won't take long to discover it's not there. Nowhere near long enough for Genia to put on makeup and perfume.

I dart into the bedroom, pull the book from its hiding place under my side of the mattress, and head for the kitchen door.

'Wait here,' I say to Zelda.

I hurry outside with the book.

This is all I can do. Give the book to the soldiers and say I'm sorry. Explain that Cyryl told me it was junk. Hope that when they see my Polish Wilhelm identity card, they'll have mercy.

At least they haven't got their killer dog with them today.

I crouch outside the door of the barn. I don't want to just barge in. Everyone knows you never creep up behind a horse or a Nazi.

I peep through a crack in the door so I can choose a moment when the soldiers haven't got their heads in the straw.

My eyes get used to the gloom and I blink with surprise and alarm.

The Nazis aren't doing a book search at all. One of them is grabbing the chickens and stuffing them into a sack. The other is putting a rope round Trotski's neck.

Trotski isn't happy. He's trying to bite the soldier. The soldier is swearing.

Genia is very upset.

'You can't take them,' she's yelling. 'You can't.'

One of the Nazi soldiers has got his gun pointed at Genia, but apart from that they're ignoring her.

Leopold is very upset too. He's barking and growling. Genia is holding him by his collar, but he's jumping and leaping, trying to get at the soldiers.

I know I should be doing the same. Or at least pleading with them.

Before I can move, I hear a voice calling out.

'Hey, Nowak.'

At first I don't understand what that means. I'm too numb to think. But slowly I realise.

That's me.

I turn round.

Cyryl and three other boys are walking towards me across the farmyard. Cyryl is grinning, but not in a friendly way. As he gets closer, I see that his face is badly bruised from when the Hitler Youth bashed him the other day.

I hurry forward to meet the boys so I can find out what they want before they get too close to the barn.

'This is my gang,' says Cyryl, pointing to the other boys, who aren't looking very friendly either.

Now I'm thinking fast. Cyryl must have decided to come here in person to report me to the Nazis for book stealing. And Zelda as well probably. So he can gloat while the Nazis arrest us. And there's nothing I can do. I've got the book in my hands. He must have seen it already.

Cyryl and the other boys come and stand very close to me. But Cyryl isn't even looking at the book.

'Do you want to join my gang?' he says.

I stare at him, surprised. I don't know what to say. I just want to get back to the barn.

'We want you to join,' says Cyryl.

The other boys all nod.

My thoughts are whirling. Maybe his gang do a lot of stealing and that's why they're inviting me. Maybe if I'm in his gang he won't press charges about the book.

'All right,' I say, stuffing the book inside my shirt.

'And me,' says another voice. 'I want to join too.'

It's Zelda. She's standing next to me, hands on her hips, looking sternly at Cyryl.

'Go back to the house,' I plead with her.

'Not unless you do,' she says.

Cyryl scowls at Zelda.

'No girls,' he says. He turns back to me. 'Before you can join, you have to do the test.'

'What test?' I say.

'Pull your trousers down,' says Cyryl.

I don't understand. But after a couple of seconds I do. Fear starts to churn inside me.

'You're rude,' says Zelda to Cyryl.

Cyryl ignores her.

'It's the entrance test for the gang,' he says to me. 'You have to prove you're not a Jew.'

My insides are quivering. I try not to show it.

'That's stupid,' I say. 'I've changed my mind. I don't want to join.'

'Too late,' says Cyryl. 'You said you did. If you don't pull your trousers down, we will.'

The other boys take a step towards me.

Cyryl is looking me right in the eye, his wet lips gleaming. I can see exactly what he's thinking.

He's hoping I've got a Jewish private part.

He can't wait to show the Nazi soldiers.

If my trousers come down, we haven't got a chance. The Nazis'll take me into town and kill me on a post. Same with Genia for hiding me. And Zelda doesn't stand a chance either. Even Nazi kids get executed if they protect Jews.

You know how when you're trapped and terrified and your insides are squeezed up with fear, you get an urgent need to do a poo?

I'm getting that now.

'Pull his trousers down,' says Cyryl.

The boys all grab at my trousers and start to undo the buttons. I try to fight them, but two of them hold my arms.

'Get off him,' yells Zelda.

Cyryl pushes her away. She sprawls onto the ground. I kick and struggle but it's no good. The boys have got two of the buttons undone already.

There's only one thing I can do. It's my last chance for us to survive.

I let the poo out.

Cyryl has got his hands on the back of my trousers, trying to drag them down.

'Urghh,' he says. 'What's that smell? Yuck, it's warm.'

I don't say anything.

He'll realise.

He does.

'Arghh,' he yells, jumping back. 'He's pooed his pants.'

The other boys jump back too.

I look down. I don't want to see their faces and what they think of me.

'Disgusting,' says one of the boys.

'Filthy maggot,' says another.

They're right, but what choice did I have?

Zelda is scrambling to her feet.

'You made him do it,' she yells at the boys. 'He doesn't usually do it.'

She puts her arms round me.

'It's not your fault,' she says. 'Sometimes poo just comes out.'

The barn door bangs open. One of the Nazi soldiers appears, carrying a sack full of squawking chickens.

Cyryl runs over to him, crowing loudly, pointing at me.

'He pooed his pants.'

Maybe he hopes the Nazi soldier will shoot me for being disgusting.

The Nazi soldier isn't in the mood. His hands and face are covered with chicken scratches. He swipes at Cyryl and almost knocks him over.

'Get lost, all of you,' he yells at us in bad Polish.

But we don't.

Cyryl stomps back towards me and I can see he's determined to get my pants down, poo or no poo.

Zelda is staring at the sack of chickens, horrified, and I can see she's determined to rescue them.

I step forward to try and stop them both.

I'm still moving forward when something else happens.

Something even worse.

Inside the barn, loud and terrible.

A gunshot.

Then we froze.

Me and Zelda and Cyryl and the other boys.

A gunshot can do that. Make your whole body go cold and rigid, even if the bullet doesn't actually hit you.

The Nazi soldier with the sack of chickens doesn't freeze. He just tosses the sack into the back of the truck. He doesn't even look concerned. He probably hears a hundred gunshots a day, most of them probably killing innocent people like Genia or innocent pigs like Trotski.

Suddenly, with a jolt of panic, I come back to life.

So do Cyryl and his gang. They stop gawking at the barn and swap scared looks.

'I haven't finished with you, Nowak,' Cyryl snarls at me, and I can see he means it.

He and the other boys sprint away.

Zelda is storming towards the chickens.

I lunge forward and grab her just as the other Nazi soldier comes out of the barn. He's putting his pistol back into its holster and dragging an angry Trotski at the end of the rope.

More panic hits me.

If it wasn't Trostski who was shot . . .

'Let that pig go,' Zelda yells at the soldiers. 'And those chickens.'

I put my hand over her mouth.

Before I can see what terrible thing has happened in the barn, I have to keep Zelda safe.

'Be a good girl, Violetta,' I say loudly, just like Genia would. 'The officers are just collecting food for the Nazi army.'

Zelda bites my hand.

I try not to let the soldiers see I'm in pain. I pretend I'm wiping dirt from round Zelda's mouth. While she grunts into my hand, I smile and wave with my other hand to the soldiers. They grunt too as they lift Trotski up and dump him in the back of the truck.

Please understand why I can't rescue you, I beg Trotski silently.

I keep smiling and waving while the Nazis drive away. It's incredibly hard, smiling with full pants and fear in your guts and an aching heart, but I do it for Zelda.

'You let them take Trotski,' Zelda yells at me when I finally take my hand off her mouth. 'You let them take the chickens.'

I try to explain but I can't speak. Zelda probably thinks it's because I'm ashamed, which I am.

But mostly it's because of what might be waiting for us in the barn.

I stop in the barn doorway, not wanting to look. From inside I hear sobbing.

A person can only sob when they're alive.

'Genia,' I whisper, weak with relief.

But my relief doesn't last long. My eyes get used to the gloom. What I see isn't a relief at all.

Leopold is lying on the ground. Not barking. Not growling. Not even moving.

Genia is kneeling next to him, her face in her hands.

'Leopold,' screams Zelda, rushing past me.

She flings herself down next to Genia and tries to lift Leopold, but his head just flops against her chest.

'Leopold,' sobs Zelda. 'Don't be dead.'

Genia looks at me and Zelda. Her eyes are red and her face is wet.

'I tried to hold him back,' she says, her voice croaky with grief. 'But his collar snapped. So they shot him.'

Now I can see how red the fur on his neck is.

Zelda is shaking with sobs, pressing her face against Leopold's limp body.

I crouch down and gently close his eyelids and stroke his soft untidy fur.

'Good boy,' I whisper.

After that I have to close my own eyes because they're so full of tears.

We bury Leopold at sunset in a corner of the cabbage field.

'It was his favourite field,' says Genia.

We lay some wild flowers and ferns onto the mound of soil.

'Why are Nazi monsters so mean and horrible?' says Zelda.

Genia and me don't reply. We don't know the answer. Instead we stand quietly by Leopold's grave and say some prayers for him.

I ask Richmal Crompton, out loud so Genia and Zelda can hear, if she can arrange for Jumble, the dog in her books, to end up in the same part of heaven as Leopold. I think they'll like each other.

'Jumble will like Trotski and the chickens too,' says Zelda.

I smile at her through my tears.

'He will,' I say.

Zelda rummages around in her coat pocket and pulls out a folded piece of paper. She unfolds it and gives it to Genia.

It's a drawing of Leopold and Trotski and the chickens all being fed automatically.

'So you can remember them,' says Zelda.

Genia looks at the drawing for a long time.

'Thank you,' she says softly. 'Both of you.'

She takes a deep breath and turns to me.

'Wilhelm,' she says.

'Yes?' I say nervously.

I'm worried about what Genia's going to say next.

While she was washing my trousers earlier she didn't say anything. Not about the poo or about how my private part nearly got us killed. But I could see her thinking about things.

What if she's decided now she simply can't protect such a dirty and dangerous boy?

Genia gives me a hug.

'I'm proud of you,' she says. 'What you did this afternoon was very brave and very quick-thinking.'

I'm a bit dazed, but glowing too.

'He can do it any time he wants,' says Zelda, hugging me from the other side. 'Any time he sees a Nazi, he can just do a poo.'

We stand with our arms round each other for a long time and I don't ever want to stop because I'm so lucky to have a family like Zelda and Genia.

Finally we walk back towards the house.

'We're going to be hungry this winter,' says Genia, looking sadly towards the barn. 'The Nazis have taken everything now. All I've got is a few cabbages and a few potatoes and a few onions.'

'And a few turnips,' says Zelda.

Genia smiles and gives her a squeeze.

'You're right, Violetta,' she says. 'We mustn't forget the turnips.'

Poor Genia. If she didn't have to feed us, at least she'd have a bit more for herself.

That's when I decide to do it.

I may not be big or tough or muscly enough to be a fighter, but there is one thing I can do.

Get more food for my family.

Then I racked my brains about where you can get food in this part of Poland with winter coming on and all the fields empty because the Nazis have stripped them bare.

Grow cabbages in the barn?

Catch birds?

Boil up acorns?

I try everything, but it's no good. You need sunlight for cabbage seeds to grow. Candles just aren't bright enough. And you can't catch birds when they've all gone to Africa to get away from the cold. And boiled acorns taste yucky and give you a belly ache.

'What about mushroom soup?' says Zelda one morning.

I look at her hopefully.

'Have you found mushrooms somewhere?' I ask.

'No,' she says, handing me a piece of paper. 'But I thought about them really hard. Like we did that time with chocolate. And I remembered what they looked like.'

I stare at a drawing of mushrooms.

'Be careful,' says Zelda sternly. 'They might be poisonous.'

In bed one night I suddenly remember the rabbit holes. That hillside me and Zelda climbed up when we were escaping from the Nazi train was full of rabbit holes.

Rabbit holes mean rabbits.

Tender juicy rabbits.

Perfect for winter stews.

I wait till Genia and Zelda are asleep. Carefully I slip out of bed. In the darkness I put on my boots. I leave my coat, I can move faster without it.

I creep into the kitchen.

I've never killed a rabbit before, so I'm not sure exactly what I'll need.

A net?

A rope to strangle them?

A knife?

I can't find a net or a rope, so I borrow Genia's vegetable knife. On my way to the door, I have another thought and I borrow her shopping bag too. It's a nice one made of string.

I'll try not to get blood on it.

I creep out of the house.

It's a cloudy night, but as I hurry across the

cabbage field, the moon comes out. The cabbage stumps gleam white in the moonlight.

Shame the rabbits don't know they're here. I bet rabbits love cabbage stumps. A field of rabbits on my doorstep would make my job a lot easier.

Well, a bit easier.

I'd still have to kill them.

'Wish me luck, Leopold,' I whisper as I pass his grave.

I'm sure he does. And I know he'd come with me if he could.

There's a chill breeze whipping across these fields, but I'll stay warm as long as I move quickly. In the distance I can see the hills, and the ragged line of forest that runs along the top. That's where the rabbit holes are, in those hills.

I try not to think about what's also there.

The poor dead children in their grave.

I reach a lane and go along it in the direction of the hills. But the lane isn't straight. It's got bends and turns. And corners. There's a high hedge on both sides and now the moon is back behind a cloud and I'm not sure any more which direction I'm going.

I leave the lane and cut across a field towards what I hope are the hills looming in front of me. I start climbing a slope. Except, as I climb, I can't see any rabbit holes. Or any trees.

Suddenly I hear voices talking loudly in the distance.

I fling myself to the ground, praying that the

moon will stay hidden so I can too. Now, as I peer ahead, I can make out a faint haze of lights.

More voices.

The growl of engines.

The moon comes out. I have to find a better hiding place than this open hillside.

I crawl up the rocky slope, hoping to find a bush or a burrow. What I see at the top is so amazing I forget all about bushes and burrows.

I even forget about rabbits.

Down the slope on the other side is a big house. About fifty times bigger than Genia's place. There's even an upstairs. Plus other buildings that look like stables or garages. Lamps are burning in just about all the rooms. A motorbike is sitting out the front with its engine running even though it's not going anywhere.

These people must be very rich.

I can see some of them, walking around outside, dark against the lit-up windows. They're talking and laughing and . . .

. . . wearing uniforms.

I wipe the sweat off my glasses and look again.

Nazis.

Now I can see trucks with swastikas on them. And guards at the gate. And machine guns.

I know I should run as far away as I can, but I can't stop looking.

I've heard how the Nazis always take the best country houses for themselves. The big ones with wine cellars and bathrooms. Which explains why they haven't moved in to Genia's place.

'Don't move.'

A voice hisses at me from behind.

I feel a cold sharp blade prick the skin on the back of my neck.

A bayonet, probably.

'Turn round,' hisses the voice. 'Slowly.'

I turn round. And find myself facing a kid.

It's a kid I've seen before. I recognise the scar on his forehead.

He's Leopold's Jewish orphan friend and he's holding the same knife as when he visited the barn. I see he has cleaned the blade. It glints in the moonlight as he points it at my chest.

He stares at me with angry, unfriendly eyes.

'How's Leopold?' he asks.

My mind races. I want to tell him the truth, but I don't want to upset him more.

'I think he's probably missing you,' I say.

I can see the kid doesn't like this answer. I wonder if I'm going to have to fight him. My knife is in my coat pocket, wrapped in Genia's shopping bag.

Even if I could get to it, I don't think it would do me much good. The kid is wearing a thick coat that reaches almost to the ground. I'm not sure a knife could stab through it.

I need to try something else.

I have an idea. It's risky, but I can't think of a less risky one.

'I'm Jewish too,' I say.

The kid doesn't move. Or lower the knife. Or stop looking at me suspiciously.

I don't really blame him. It's very hard to trust people in the modern world. I need to give him some proof.

'Don't be alarmed,' I say. 'I'm going to pull my trousers down.'

He doesn't even blink.

Very slowly, so he can see there's no trick involved, I pull my trousers down.

The kid looks at my private part.

'What's your name?' he says.

'Felix,' I say. 'But I'm pretending to be Wilhelm.'

There. I've said it. Now he's got two ways to kill me. He can stab me, or he can tell the Nazis I'm Jewish.

'What's yours?' I say.

The kid doesn't answer. But he lowers the knife.

'What are you doing here?' he says.

'Hunting rabbits,' I say as I pull my trousers up. 'I got lost. What are you doing here?'

For a few moments he looks like he's not going to answer that question either. But he does.

'I come here a lot,' he says quietly. 'I used to live here.'

My mind races again. This big house must have been the Jewish orphanage. The one the Nazis wanted empty so the Hitler Youth could move in.

Poor kid.

All his friends murdered.

We both stare down at the house. I can't see any Hitler Youth here at the moment. They must be in bed. But there are several Nazi soldiers and officers strutting around, wasting lamp oil and not caring about the dead children they shot last month.

Suddenly I want revenge.

I want to do something to them that will make them go back to Germany and never shoot another dog or child or hang another grown-up from a post ever again.

Something that will hurt them a lot.

I take deep breaths and tell myself to stop being silly. Who am I kidding? What could one boy do with a vegetable knife and a shopping bag?

Even two boys with two knives.

I turn away.

Anyway, I say to myself, we're not like them. We only kill for food.

Suddenly I remember Leopold's rabbit meat. This kid must know how to hunt rabbits.

'Hey,' I say to him. 'Lets go hunting.'

The kid shakes his head, not taking his eyes off the Nazis in the orphanage.

I get the feeling he doesn't mind the idea of hunting, just not with me.

Then I asked the kid more questions like where was he from originally and how did he escape being shot with the other orphans and where is he living now but he won't answer so I say goodbye and head off to hunt rabbits.

On my own.

When I finally make it to the forest, I stand in among the dark trees, wondering which way the railway line is.

Richmal Crompton hears my prayers. She helps me choose the right direction.

Also a train clatters past in the distance to give me an extra clue.

I crouch in the ferns, looking down at the hillside covered in rabbit holes. The moon is out and so are the rabbits, peeking out of their tunnels as the sound of the train dies away.

I check that the vegetable knife and the shopping bag are still in my pocket.

This is going to be the difficult part.

Catching a wild rabbit will be hard. I'll have to be very fast.

Cutting its throat will be even harder. I'll have to try and make myself into a killer. Just for a few seconds. For my family.

All right . . .

Here goes . . .

I plunge my hands into a rabbit hole.

Oh no. I've got one. A live rabbit, kicking and struggling in my arms. Warm and quivering. I slide my hand up to its throat and reach for the knife. I can feel the veins in its throat throbbing and now it's looking at me with big dark eyes . . .

What was that?

Gunshots.

I've been seen.

I drop the rabbit and dive back into the thick ferns, waiting for bullets to smash into me, imagining Zelda waking up not knowing where I've gone, never finding out why I didn't come back, thinking I broke my promise.

The shooting stops.

The rabbits have all dived for cover too, except for a few who are twitching and dying.

Voices boom out from the trees. Nazi soldiers, several of them, with torches and guns, slide and slither their way down the slope. They pick up the dead rabbits and examine them in the torchlight.

I'm almost weeping with relief.

It wasn't me they were after.

But that's not the only reason I'm relieved. I can still feel that rabbit's veins, throbbing frantically. My head is throbbing now in just the same way.

I couldn't have killed it.

Not even to feed my family.

I don't know how Leopold's friend can do it.

I stay hidden and watch the soldiers. I can't understand what they're saying, but their voices don't sound very happy. I'm not surprised. There are four of them and only three dead rabbits.

As they climb back up the hillside, they're arguing about something.

Suddenly I understand one of the words.

Fische.

It's one of the few German words I know. When I was little, a German tourist came into our bookshop and asked where he could catch fish in our local river and Dad told him.

The Nazi soldiers seem to be agreeing about *Fische* now.

I think it sounds like a good idea too. I think I'll be better at catching fish than killing rabbits.

The Nazi soldiers head off through the forest.

I follow them.

I didn't know there was a river in these parts.

It's not as big as the river I grew up near, but it's big enough for fish, I can see that even from behind these bushes.

The Nazi soldiers are standing on the river bank. One of them is fiddling with something in a bag. I wonder what it is? The bag doesn't look big enough for a fishing rod.

Suddenly the soldier throws something, a dark lump, and it splashes into the river.

They can't be trying to kill fish with rocks, that's crazy. Perhaps they're using rabbit meat as bait.

The other soldiers duck.

An explosion erupts out of the water.

A huge one.

I'm deafened and drenched even over here. As I wipe the water off my face and glasses, my dazed mind tries to make sense of what's happening. Is this a battle? Are we being bombed?

The Nazi soldiers are all in the river, yelling excitedly and waving fish at each other. I can see other fish floating in the water.

Now I get it.

They're fishing. That thing they chucked into the river must have been one of those bombs you throw with your hand, what's it called . . .

'Hand grenade,' says a voice in my ear.

I nearly pass out with shock.

It's Leopold's friend, crouching next to me in the bushes. He must have crept up while the hand grenade was going off.

'Keep your head down,' he mutters.

We watch the soldiers splash around, gathering up dead fish and tossing them onto the shore.

Silently I beg them to leave a couple for me and Zelda and Genia. And one for the kid.

'You still want to go hunting?' says the kid quietly. 'You and me?'

I look at him, surprised. Does he mean fish or rabbits?

I nod uncertainly.

The kid reaches into the big pockets of his coat and pulls out a few things and puts them on the ground in front of us.

The first thing I see is his knife.

There's blood on it again.

But it's the other two things that really shock me. Guns.

Two big dark shiny hand guns.

I stare at them. The kid picks one up and holds it out to me. I don't know what to say.

'W-what are we hunting?' I stammer.

The kid doesn't answer. Just squints at the Nazi soldiers, who are still gathering up stunned and dead fish.

I feel like a stunned fish myself.

Does he mean . . .?

I stare him. He can't mean that. We're kids.

He looks at me, waiting.

After a few moments he gives a snort and puts the weapons back in his pocket.

'Forget it,' he says, and disappears into the dark undergrowth.

Suddenly I want to get out of here.

But the soldiers haven't finished yet. They clamber out of the water and the one with the bag grabs another grenade. He throws it into the river. The other three soldiers put their hands over their ears and turn away.

I'm about to do the same when I see something near the grenade-throwing Nazi that makes me freeze, even though I know I'm about to be deafened and blinded again.

The kid.

He's stepping out from behind a tree.

Holding one of the guns in both hands.

Pointing it at the back of the Nazi's head.

I stop breathing.

For a moment everything else seems to stop. But only for a moment. Now the water is exploding again, as loud as before.

'Don't,' I yell at the kid.

But I can't hear my own voice, so I'm sure he can't either.

The kid's arms twitch and the Nazi soldier falls forward onto the river bank.

My head is ringing and my glasses are covered with spray. The kid is just a blur now, but he seems to be bending down, reaching for something.

When I finish wiping my glasses, he's gone.

So has the grenade bag.

The other Nazis see their friend on the ground. They run to him, shouting at him and at each other and turning him over.

I've only got a few seconds before they realise it wasn't the grenade that got him. A few seconds before they start hunting for a culprit.

I run.

Then I realised that running was stupid.

Soon the whole area will be full of troops looking for the kid who killed the Nazi soldier. There'll be dogs. Trucks. Maybe even planes.

I stop running. I have a better idea. I'll hide in the one place they probably won't look.

The river.

I'm a fair way along the river bank from the dead Nazi. I find a place where low branches dip into the water. I slide down the muddy bank under the leaves.

This is a good hiding place. The water is up to my chin and the branches hide my head from view. Only two things worry me, apart from being found and killed. The water is very cold and Genia's good shopping bag is very wet.

The minutes tick by, lots of them. After a while I can hear troops and trucks and dogs. I pass the time thinking about the kid.

How could he do it?

Shoot another person in the head?

I couldn't even kill a rabbit.

He must be very strong and very determined. And very stupid. Doesn't he know that Nazis will do anything for revenge? Didn't he stop and think that he was putting every child for miles around in serious danger?

Leopold could have told him.

I think about Zelda, sleeping peacefully and not even knowing that by tomorrow she could be on a Nazi revenge death list.

A dead fish floats towards me, eyes dull in the moonlight.

'I won't let them get her,' I say to the fish.

The fish doesn't reply, but it doesn't need to. I know what I'm going to do.

I wait until the trucks and the dogs have finally gone and I pull myself and the fish out of the water and start heading back to Genia's.

The sky is clear now. The air is cold. I move fast so I don't freeze.

With the help of the moon and Richmal Crompton and the distant engine sounds of trucks being parked, I manage to avoid the Hitler Youth orphanage.

I find the lane.

I find Leopold's cabbage field.

I'm feeling tired and exhausted as well as cold and wet, but the sun will probably be up in a couple of hours so I don't have any time to waste.

I hurry into the barn. Genia doesn't bother keeping it locked now that Trotski and the chickens are gone.

Inside the barn I put the fish down, take my wet clothes off, find a spade and start digging.

'Wilhelm, what are you doing?'

You know how when you've been working on a hole for ages and you've got used to only hearing the sound of the digging, chunk, chunk, chunk, and suddenly somebody startles you and you nearly slice into your foot with the spade?

That just happened to me.

'Wilhelm,' says Genia sternly. 'What is going on?'

I look up. She's standing at the edge of the hole in her nightdress and coat. The early morning sun is milky through the open barn door behind her.

Now I've stopped digging, I realise the hole is getting quite big. I'm standing in it and only my head is above ground level.

Good.

It's nearly deep enough.

'Come out of there,' says Genia, frowning.

I can see she's wondering why I'm naked.

She reaches down and grabs my hand and hauls me up. Now that I'm standing next to her, even through my sweaty glasses I can see what a mess I've made. Dirt is scattered all around the barn.

'Sorry,' I say. 'I'll clean it up.'

Genia is staring at me with the expression people get when somebody has dug a hole in the floor of their barn and they don't understand why.

'It's for Zelda,' I explain. 'I mean Violetta. An emergency hiding place. In case the Nazis come for her. I've made it big enough so she can lie down. We can put straw in the bottom and Leopold's kennel over the top.'

I stop talking to give Genia a chance to take it all in.

She's looking at me as if she thinks I'm a bit mad. Oh well, at least she's not staring at my private part. And she won't think the hole is a crazy idea when I tell her about the killer kid at the river.

But before I can, Genia speaks first.

'Wilhelm,' she says softly. 'It's a very kind idea, but think about it. Can you honestly imagine Violetta staying still and quiet and hidden for more than two minutes? You know what a fidget she is.'

A chill runs through me, even though I'm hot and dripping with sweat.

I hadn't thought of that.

'I'm not a fidget,' says an indignant voice. 'I'm just lively. Don't you know anything?'

Zelda is standing in the doorway, rubbing her eyes sleepily. She comes to the edge of the hole and looks down into it.

'It's too small,' she says. 'Only one person can hide in there, not two of us.'

I hadn't thought of that either. I forgot about

me. My brain must be addled because I haven't slept all night.

Zelda's face is a mixture of crossness and such loving concern that I want to hug her.

I don't because I'm covered in sweat and mud. And Genia is staring at my pile of wet clothes. And the fish. And the things from the kitchen. She's looking like she might explode.

'Wilhelm,' she says quietly. 'Have you been to the river?'

I nod.

I can see from her face she's struggling to control herself. Probably because she doesn't know whether she should thank me for getting food or yell at me for getting her shopping bag wet.

I confess everything. The rabbits. The Nazis fishing with grenades. Leopold's killer friend.

When I've finished, Genia doesn't speak for a long time.

Zelda does.

'I want Leopold's friend to teach me how to do it,' she says quietly as she stares at Leopold's kennel. 'How to shoot a Nazi.'

Genia gives her a look.

Zelda sticks out her bottom lip, stubborn and determined.

'The Nazis will take revenge for tonight,' says Genia. 'People will die. But if you really did get away without being seen, Wilhelm, there's no reason any of us will suffer.'

I sag with relief.

'I did,' I say.

'Good,' says Genia. 'I want you to promise me you'll never do anything like that again.'

I think about how upset I felt when the kid shot the Nazi and how cold I was in the river and how worried I've been ever since.

'I promise,' I say.

Genia nods. I can see she believes me.

'If the Nazis come for revenge,' says Zelda, 'I'll shoot them.'

Genia frowns. I think she's starting to see the problem we have with Zelda and Nazis.

Then Genia and Zelda went out while I was sleeping and found some delicious herbs and made a fish stew.

It's the best one I've ever tasted. The last one was about six years ago, but Mum only had caraway seeds for herbs and I didn't like the taste of them much. I could probably get to like them now, though. If Genia can get to like Jewish people, anything's possible.

'Would you like some more stew?' says Genia.

'Yes, please,' I say.

There's nothing like a herb and fish stew to stop you worrying about Nazi revenge attacks. For a while, anyway.

'Yes, please, thank you very much,' says Zelda.

Genia goes over to the stove to get the pot.

Zelda is making a picture on the table with her fish bones. Little stick figures with fish-bone arms and legs. They look happy.

I wish Genia looked happy. She's been frowning and biting her lip ever since she got back with the herbs. I hope she's not having regrets about using all the fish in the stew instead of saving some.

She could have preserved some of the fish with salt and stored it in the wardrobe like I suggested. Preserving is a really good way of keeping food for winter. Mum used to do it with carrots. I bet in the future they invent lots of ways of preserving food. I bet by the year 1970 we'll be able to eat cherries in winter if we want, or lettuce.

Genia gives a big sigh.

On a second thoughts I think she's worried about something more important than preserved fish. I think she's worried about Zelda, like me.

I look at Zelda's fish-bone figures again. Both of them have got fish-bone smiles. I'm glad she's doing a happy picture.

'Is that your real mummy and daddy?' I say to her.

As usual I'm hoping it is. The sooner she gives up this crazy idea that she's Jewish, the less likely she'll have to use the emergency hole in the barn.

'Your mummy and daddy look happy,' I say to Zelda. 'I know why. It's because they've still got you as their daughter and they love you very much. Love is like preserved carrot. It never goes off.'

'Wilhelm's right,' says Genia quietly. 'A person doesn't have to be here to love you.'

Zelda puts fish-bone whiskers on the faces of her figures.

'They're rabbits,' she says to me. 'They're happy because you didn't stab them.'

I sigh. I'm happy I didn't stab them. But I'd be happier if Zelda could forgive her parents.

I glance over at Genia. She's still at the stove. She's staring at the photo of her husband she keeps in a frame on the shelf.

She's been staring at it a lot today.

Suddenly I realise why she's unhappy.

Of course. Here's me so worried about Zelda, I'm forgetting Genia's got someone she cares about just as much.

'You must really miss him,' I say to her.

Genia looks at me with a guilty expression, like she didn't want me to see her staring at the photo.

'Yes,' she says.

Poor Genia. She hasn't seen her husband for two years. She must be missing him a huge amount.

'I had some news about him today,' Genia says.

I feel a jolt of concern. It couldn't have been good news, not with her looking so worried.

'Has something bad happened to him?' I say, hoping I'm wrong.

'No,' says Genia. 'Nothing bad.'

I feel relieved. Except why is she looking so miserable?

Genia comes over with the stew pot and puts it on the table. She looks at me and Zelda as she slowly spoons more fish stew into our bowls.

'You know I told you how Gabriek was forced to go to Germany to work for the Nazis?' she says.

I nod.

Zelda glares indignantly. 'Nazis shouldn't force people,' she says.

'He's coming home,' says Genia. 'Probably in a few days.'

At first I'm happy for her. And for her husband.

'Hooray,' yells Zelda, clapping her hands.

But Genia isn't cheering or clapping. She isn't even smiling.

I don't get it.

Why wouldn't a person be happy that her husband is coming home? I can only think of two possible reasons. Either she doesn't like him any more, or she's worried about what will happen when he gets here.

I can't sleep.

It's partly because I slept for half the day. And also because I'm worried.

Zelda can't sleep either. I can feel her tossing and turning next to me in the darkness.

'Don't fidget,' I whisper to her. 'You'll drag the covers off Genia.'

'I'm not fidgeting,' whispers Zelda, turning over again. 'I'm thinking.'

Luckily Genia is a deep sleeper because Zelda is the noisiest thinker I know.

'Felix,' says Zelda. 'After Genia's husband gets here, will there be enough food for us all?'

'Don't worry,' I say. 'I'm sure there'll be enough. He can help us get more if we need it.'

Zelda is so clever. Only six and she's thinking about grown-up things like that. I'm ten, so it's natural for me to worry. Specially now I know the real reason Genia is so unhappy.

Genia told me earlier, when I was helping her clear up.

'It's all right,' she said to me. 'Gabriek won't mind you being here. It'll be fine.'

That's all she said but I know what she meant.

Genia's worried that when her husband gets back and sees what the Nazis are doing to people who protect Jews, he might think it's too risky for me and Zelda to stay here.

Too risky for him and Genia.

I haven't said anything to Zelda yet. I don't want to worry her. Little kids should be protected from worry as much as possible. Now that Leopold and Trotski and the chickens have gone, poor Zelda hasn't got anything to take her mind off the war except for one pencil and some fish bones.

I close my eyes and try to think of a good side to Gabriek coming home.

For example, if he doesn't throw us out, Zelda will be able to see him and Genia being loving to each other and that might bring back happy memories of her real mum and dad.

That makes me feel better.

I'm not going to think any more negative thoughts about Gabriek.

I peer at Zelda in the gloom to see if she's getting sleepy.

She's still awake, and she's frowning.

'Felix,' she says. 'After Genia's husband gets here, what if he doesn't want us?'

Then the next day dawned, and the one after that, and quite a few more, and Genia's husband didn't arrive.

'He must be having trouble with his travel arrangements,' I say to Zelda.

We feel sorry for Genia, but relieved as well. We stay feeling relieved right up until the next morning, when the local police come round to all the farms with strict instructions.

Everybody be in the town square at ten o'clock on the dot.

By order of the Nazis.

We don't want to go, but we have to.

Everyone does.

We're all very gloomy as we trudge into town. It's drizzling and the road is muddy and the wind is cold. Me and Zelda and Genia have got our coats and hats on. Mrs Placzek is wearing two headscarves. She's so gloomy she doesn't even say hello, just stares down at the road as she walks past us.

This makes me feel worried. When you're a Jew in hiding and somebody stops being friendly, it could be serious. Or maybe Mrs Placzek is just worried like us. Maybe she doesn't know either why the Nazis want us in the town square.

'Genia, why are the Nazis making us be in town?' says Zelda for the hundredth time.

'Don't worry, Violetta,' replies Genia, also for the hundredth time. 'It'll be fine.'

But she doesn't look very sure.

Earlier, as we were leaving the house, Zelda whispered to me that maybe everyone was going to town to have a party to welcome Genia's husband home.

I told her I didn't think so. I also told her that he might not be home for a while yet because Germany is a long way away.

That cheered her up a bit.

Me too, for a couple of minutes. But now I'm worried again. Why do the Nazis want us in town? Revenge for what happened at the river?

I'm also worried we might bump into Cyryl and his gang. Even if the Nazis don't want revenge, I know Cyryl does.

'Genia,' says Zelda. 'Will the Nazis make us go shopping in town?'

Genia gives a big sigh, which can sometimes mean she's getting cross.

'I might as well tell you,' she says. 'You'll find out sooner or later. They're making us go there to mock Jews.'

Genia's right. That is why we're here.

Nazi soldiers and local police and Hitler Youth are making everyone stand on both sides of the town square. They're making us look at a straggling line of Jewish people shuffling past us.

I can tell the people are Jewish because they're all wearing white armbands with a blue star. The star reminds me of the one Mum has on her plate for special cakes.

Used to have, I mean.

I'm feeling very sad because these poor people are so thin and pale and their clothes are so ragged. A lot of them look ill. I don't know how they can walk. Specially the old people and the little kids. They probably wouldn't be walking at all if the Nazi soldiers weren't yelling at them and hitting them.

'Murdering Nazi scum,' mutters Genia softly, so only me and Zelda can hear.

'Where are those people going?' says Zelda in a loud concerned voice.

A man standing next to us chuckles in a not very nice way.

'Railway station,' he says. 'One way ticket to somewhere hot. And I don't mean Africa.'

I know where he means. A death camp where the Nazis burn people up after they kill them.

Some of the people around us are laughing. Others are disgusted. I'm not sure if they're disgusted with the man, or because some of the Jewish people are being sick onto the cobbles.

'Filthy vermin,' the man yells at the poor straggling prisoners.

So do quite a few other people.

I don't understand. Why do the Nazis want us to mock and insult the Jewish people? Aren't the Jewish people suffering enough?

I wish we could help them.

I wish we could at least give them some food or clothes from Mrs Szynsky's shop or something.

Genia nudges me.

'Shout at them, Wilhelm,' she whispers.

For a second I don't know what she means. Nazi soldiers are glaring at us and making it hard for me to think.

'Filthy vermin,' Genia yells at the Jewish people.

I'm not exactly sure what vermin are, but I can tell from the fierce look on Genia's face that it's not a nice thing to call people. I'm shocked until I see how sad her eyes are. Suddenly I realise why she's doing it and why she wants me to do it as well.

It's to make us look like we hate Jews, specially me.

'Go on,' Genia hisses at me and Zelda.

I can see Zelda doesn't want to. I can see from her frown that she wants to go home. But she can't because Genia is holding her hand very tight.

I'm worried by Zelda's frown. If she loses her temper, I know what will happen. She'll yell out something that will make the Nazis think that neither of us hates Jews.

I have to do it.

I take a deep breath, and I try not to look at any of the Jewish people, and I do my best.

'Filthy vermin,' I yell, but suddenly I'm thinking of Mum and Dad and their journey to their death camp and my voice goes wobbly and my eyes fill with tears and I wish I could be like Leopold's friend and point a gun at all the laughing faces and pull the trigger and . . .

I shut my eyes and make the thoughts go away.

I tell myself to think of Zelda.

I remind myself I must never do anything to put her in danger.

When I've calmed down, I open my eyes.

I'm too ashamed to look at the Jewish people. I look over their heads. That doesn't really help because now I'm staring at all the dead people hanging from the wooden posts. There are lots of them because the Nazis did take revenge for what happened at the river.

I look in another direction. And see somebody I recognise. Standing near us with his back to the Jewish people, helping the other Nazis supervise the onlookers, is the Hitler Youth boy who spotted my Richmal Crompton book.

Except he's not doing much supervising.

He's staring off into the distance like I was trying to do. He doesn't look stern and enthusiastic like the other Nazis, he looks sad.

'Filthy vermin,' yells Genia loudly.

I tell myself she's shouting it at the Nazis rather than at the Jews.

The Hitler Youth boy must have heard her, because he glances over. And sees me. And now he's coming over.

Is he going to bash me for not mocking the Jewish people enough?

No, he's grinning.

'Richmal Crompton,' he says to me. 'My favourite.'

I'm stunned. I've never met a Nazi Richmal Crompton fan before. Plus he speaks Polish with quite a good accent.

'Good stories,' says the Hitler Youth boy, still smiling. 'Very funny.'

I nod. I'm trying to smile back, but behind the Hitler Youth boy I can see a Jewish man and a Jewish woman, their thin arms round each other, helping each other stagger along.

They look like they're in so much pain.

Somebody pushes past me.

'Violetta,' I hear Genia yell frantically. 'Come back.'

I turn to see what Zelda's doing.

Genia must have been distracted by the Nazi Richmal Crompton fan too, because Zelda has pulled away from her and is darting past the Nazi supervisors.

She goes up to the Jewish man and woman.

'My mummy and daddy are dead,' she says to them. 'If you want, you can be their replacements.'

The man and the woman stare at her.

So do I. She learned that word replacements from me and I wish she hadn't.

'If you be my new mummy and daddy,' Zelda says to the man and woman, 'you can come and live with me and Wilhelm and our aunty Genia and you won't have to go to the hot place.'

A Nazi soldier grabs Zelda with one hand and raises his rifle.

He's going to smash her in the head with it.

I fling myself forward.

'No,' I shout. 'She's only little. She doesn't mean any harm.'

I'm scrabbling in my coat for Zelda's locket to show the Nazi she's one of them. But the pockets are full of fluff and my frantic fingers can't find it.

The Nazi soldier turns angrily to me and before I can plead any more, he jabs his rifle butt down and my head explodes.

Then I opened my eyes and I wasn't dead.

Just home.

In bed.

In pain.

Genia is staring down at me. Her face is shiny and worried in the daylight that's jabbing through the window.

'Thank God,' she says.

'Where's Zelda?' I croak.

It's all coming back to me. Zelda talking to the Jewish couple. Being grabbed by a Nazi. Did she get bashed too? Or worse?

Zelda's face pops up next to Genia's.

'I'm here,' she says. 'Don't you know anything?'

She looks fine, as far as I can see. I can't see very clearly because my head is throbbing and every time it does the whole room flickers.

I look around for my glasses. They're next to the bed and they don't seem to be broken.

'Are you injured?' Genia asks me anxiously. 'Can you move your arms and legs?'

I move everything a bit. When I do, my head hurts more.

'It's just my head,' I murmur.

'You were knocked out,' says Zelda. 'You came home in a cart.'

Genia is dabbing at my head with a damp cloth, which feels cool and soothing and very painful.

I squint at Zelda, trying to see if she has any injuries. She's very brave for her age and she might be hiding them so Genia won't be worried.

'Thanks for trying to rescue me,' says Zelda, squeezing my hand.

'Are you all right?' I say to her.

Zelda nods.

'Violetta's not hurt,' says Genia. 'Thanks to your Hitler Youth friend. He persuaded the soldier who hit you to let Violetta go.'

'He was nice,' says Zelda. 'He wasn't a murdering Nazi scum.'

I say a silent thank you to the Hitler Youth boy, whatever his name is. And to Richmal Crompton.

Genia is double-checking my arms and legs. She looks at me, puzzled.

'How do you know that German boy?' she says.

'We like the same books,' I say.

'Richmal Crompton books,' says Zelda. 'Richmal Crompton is English, but we don't mind.'

I lift my head off the pillow and squint at Genia,

trying to see if she minds that I've got a Nazi friend. Grown-ups can sometimes go straight from being anxious to being cross when they realise kids aren't badly hurt.

She doesn't seem to mind.

I hope she's not cross with Zelda either.

'Violetta didn't mean to cause trouble,' I explain to Genia. 'What she said to that Jewish couple about being replacements, she got that idea from me.'

'It's all right,' says Genia gently. 'Violetta and I have talked about it. I'd have offered those poor people shelter myself if it was possible.'

'Our bed's not big enough,' says Zelda.

I flop back, relieved.

Genia dabs my head again.

'It's stopped bleeding,' she says. 'I don't think it'll need stitches. But you will have a big bruise.'

Zelda leans over and kisses my head.

'That's good for bruises,' she says.

'Thanks,' I say.

'Come on, Violetta,' says Genia. 'We have to let Wilhelm rest.' She looks at me again, still worried. 'Are you feeling any better?'

'Yes,' I say. 'I am.'

But it's not true.

I'm feeling worse. Not because of my throbbing head, because of the thoughts I'm having.

I try to make the thoughts go away. I try to sleep instead. But every time I hear Zelda's voice in the kitchen, the thoughts come back.

I'm thinking about how that Nazi soldier probably wouldn't have let Zelda go if he'd seen my private part. How he'd have assumed she was Jewish like me and shot us both.

I'm also having thoughts about how Genia's husband might let a non-Jewish kid live here, just not a Jewish one.

Thoughts about how Zelda will never be safe while I'm around.

Just thinking that makes a pain stab inside me worse than a hundred bayonets.

But it's true.

She won't.

I know now what I have to do. I've been pretending for ages that I don't have to do it, but I do.

It's what Mum and Dad did for me when they hid me in that Catholic orphanage. They didn't want to do it, but they had to. They went away and left me and stopped being with me to keep me safe.

That's what I have to do for Zelda.

I ask Richmal Crompton to help me have the strength to do it.

Richmal Crompton lets me cry for a while, because that can be a part of getting strength.

After I wipe my eyes, she helps me think about things. About how she's with me every day, in my thoughts and in my imagination, even though she's not actually physically here.

I can be with Zelda like that.

In her thoughts.

In her imagination.

After I've gone.

But first I have to make sure Zelda doesn't enrage any more Nazi thugs.

I'm still trying to get her to draw a happy picture of her real parents. So she'll feel better about them. So she won't hate Nazis so much in public. So she won't tell any more nutty stories about being Jewish.

'No,' says Zelda, scowling.

She flings the pencil down and throws herself onto the bed next to me.

The bed wobbles, which hurts my head, but I try not to show it. Genia only let Zelda come in here because I said I was feeling better after a sleep.

I think Genia knows now how important Zelda's feeling about her parents are. That's why she bought Zelda a new pencil.

'Let me have a go,' I say to Zelda.

I prop myself up and put my glasses on and squint at the wrinkled shop paper and draw a picture of Zelda's parents helping her look after a sick chicken.

In the picture Zelda is bandaging the chicken's head. Her mum and dad are holding the aspirin and lemonade.

'They were very kind, your mummy and daddy,' I say as I show Zelda the picture.

'Goebbels wasn't a boy chicken,' says Zelda. 'She was a girl chicken.'

I make Goebbels a girl chicken.

'That's not my mummy and daddy being kind,' says Zelda. 'That's Violetta's mummy and daddy being kind.'

She takes the pencil and draws two tiny figures on the horizon.

'Who's that?' I say.

'Don't you know anything?' says Zelda. 'That's my Nazi mummy and daddy. Shooting children.'

I sigh and my head hurts and not just because of the bruise.

I have to accept it. This plan isn't working. I need another way to keep Zelda safe after I've gone.

I ask Richmal Crompton to help me find another way.

While I'm waiting for her to get back to me, I light the lamp next to the bed and read myself a story from her book.

It's to help with the pain.

Not my head pain, the other one, the leaving-Zelda pain.

Except I'm finding it hard to concentrate. I'm reading each page three times and I'm still not sure what this story's about. I'm on the last page now and I haven't got a clue why William and his friends are throwing onions and potatoes out of his bedroom window at a grown-up.

It's no good. I'm too miserable for a story. And I've still got the sad pain in my chest.

Wait a minute.

Potatoes . . .

Reading about potatoes is reminding me of something Genia was talking about recently.

Something that might help protect Zelda.

Yes.

Richmal Crompton, thank you.

I climb high into the tree and don't fall out.

This is good.

If you can climb a tree only two days after being bashed on the head by a Nazi, you know he hasn't done any permanent damage.

I look out across the potato field.

Lots of people are bent over the furrows, picking potatoes and putting them in baskets. Adults as well as kids.

This is what Genia was talking about. The Nazis haven't got any orphans left to pick the potatoes, so now they're making people from town do it.

Genia was right about something else too.

The potato pickers aren't just being guarded by grown-up Nazis, they're being guarded by Hitler Youth as well.

I peer down at the Hitler Youth boys in the potato field.

Please, I beg Richmal Crompton, let your fan be on potato duty. And please let me spot him quickly because I have to get home. Genia and Zelda will be back from their rabbit hunt soon and I'm not meant to be out of bed.

Yes.

There he is.

The only Hitler Youth Richmal Crompton fan in the whole world, supervising the potato pickers with his Hitler Youth mates. I'm pleased to see he's not swaggering quite as much as the others.

Excellent.

Tomorrow I'll get myself rounded up to do potato picking. Which will give me the whole day to have a quiet word with him.

I won't feel so bad if I know Zelda's got some Nazi protection after I've gone.

Then the next day I told Genia a lie. I told her I felt too ill to go rabbit hunting with her and Zelda. I told her I needed to stay in bed.

But I didn't.

After they left, I got up and put my Richmal Crompton book in my coat pocket and walked into town and waited to be rounded up for potato picking.

The potato trucks are in the town square now. The Nazi soldiers are ordering us to get onto them.

People don't like having to do potato picking for the Nazis, but most people don't try to run away. It's only for a few hours and it's better than being shot.

I clamber up onto a truck. I try to look annoyed like the other people I'm squeezed in here with. But not too annoyed. People who look like trouble-makers get hit.

I'm not here to make trouble, I'm here to help Zelda.

I know this is risky, letting the Nazis round me up, what with my private part and everything. But it's a risk I have to take. And I've got an emergency plan. I stopped myself doing a poo this morning in case I need it later.

As the truck jolts and rumbles along the road out of town, I spot the person I've come to see.

The Richmal Crompton fan. He's in a jeep with some other Hitler Youth. They speed past our truck and head towards the front of the convoy. The Richmal Crompton fan doesn't see me because I'm jammed in with so many other people, but that doesn't matter.

I've got all day.

Now there's only one other person I have to keep my eyes open for.

Cyryl.

I didn't see him in the town square, and he's not on this truck, and I don't think he's on any of the others.

So far so good.

You know how when you're doing potato picking for the Nazis and you're desperate to be seen by one particular Hitler Youth boy but he's over the other side of the field and you daren't go over to him because potato pickers have to stay in their own furrow so you pray to Richmal Crompton for help and she makes it rain?

That's happening now.

We're all running for shelter under the trees.

The Nazis don't do potato picking in the rain. They don't like the potatoes to get too wet because soggy potatoes go mushy when they're stored. I don't think they have recipes for mushy potatoes in German cooking.

I see the Richmal Crompton fan standing under a tree chatting with some other Hitler Youth. I go and stand under the next tree.

He hasn't seen me yet.

'Jew!'

Oh no.

Someone else has.

I know that voice.

Cyryl.

He must have been on one of the other trucks. Now he's pointing at me, his face pink with anger and his wet lips shining.

'This rat is a Jew,' he yells. 'Check his willy. I bet I'm right.'

I hear several loud clicks. I realise what the sound is. Nazi soldiers releasing the safety catches on their guns.

One of the soldiers puts his gun down and comes towards me. I see why he wants both hands free. He's planning to undo my trouser buttons.

I push hard in my guts.

The poo won't come.

It should come out easily because I'm terrified, but it's not coming out at all.

I must be too terrified.

I strain my guts one more time.

Nothing.

My insides are in a knot of panic. Suddenly I think of something else to try. My last hope. I stuff my hand in my coat pocket and feel around frantically under the Richmal Crompton book.

Yes.

Zelda's locket.

I pull it out and hold it up in front of the Nazi soldier. He takes it and looks at it, frowning. The other soldiers and Hitler Youth boys crowd round and peer at it too.

Please, I beg silently. Please think Zelda's parents are my parents.

The soldier holding the locket says something to me in Nazi, which I don't understand.

I panic even more. Will this give me away? If I was a real Nazi kid, even a Polish one, I should be able to understand some German.

There's only one person here who can help me.

I take the Richmal Crompton book from my pocket and hold it so the Hitler Youth boy can see it and remember who I am.

For a few seconds we stare at each other, but only for a few seconds.

The Hitler Youth boy steps forward, says something to the soldier in German, and turns to me.

'Listen carefully,' he says to me in Polish. 'The sergeant is asking you if the people in the locket are members of your family.'

I feel dizzy with gratitude.

'Yes,' I say. 'They are.'

Zelda is my family, so her parents must be too, sort of.

The Hitler Youth boy turns back to the soldiers and speaks to them again in German. He says a lot of things. The soldiers nod. Whatever he's telling them, they look like they're believing it. They lower their guns.

'He's a Jew,' yells Cyryl. 'He stole that book from my family's shop.'

The Hitler Youth boy steps over to Cyryl and punches him hard in the stomach. Cyryl keels over, clutching himself.

The Nazi soldiers and the other Hitler Youth all laugh and clap.

I look away.

I should feel glad that Cyryl's been punished. But I don't. In my experience, punches in the stomach just make enemies into bigger enemies.

The sergeant hands me Zelda's locket. He turns and starts shouting. You don't have to speak German to know what he's saying. It's stopped raining. We have to go back to work.

'My name's Amon,' says the Hitler Youth boy as we walk back to my furrow.

'I'm Wilhelm,' I say.

For a second I'm tempted to tell him my real name, but that would be crazy.

Amon smiles.

'Your parents must really like Richmal Crompton,' he says. 'To give you the same name as her hero.'

I nod. I feel guilty lying to Amon after he's saved my life, so I tell him as much of the truth as I can.

'My parents liked the William stories a lot,' I say. 'They used to read to me every night. But they're dead now.'

Amon gives me a sympathetic look.

The sergeant's still yelling. I know I haven't got much time to talk, so I say what I've come to say.

'Amon, I have to go away soon. After I've gone, will you look out for my sister Violetta like you did the other day? Sometimes she says things that aren't true. Things that upset your army.'

Amon thinks about this.

For a while I worry he's going to ask me why I have to go away. But he doesn't.

'Tell Violetta,' he says, 'if she gets into trouble, to ask for me. Amon Kurtz.'

'Thank you,' I say, weak with relief.

'The SS officers know me,' he says. 'I speak Polish. I translate for them sometimes when they're having drinks with women.'

I hold my William book out to Amon.

'This is for you,' I say.

He looks surprised. And pleased.

'Thank you,' he says.

Amon takes the book and looks at it for a moment. His face goes serious. He glances around the potato field to make sure nobody else is listening.

'I wish Richmal Crompton was in charge of Germany instead of Adolf Hitler,' he says quietly. 'If she was, I wouldn't have to be in the Hitler Youth. You and me, we'd both be at home with our parents. I wouldn't be sleeping in a dead kid's bed.'

He puts the book inside his jacket.

I want to talk with him more, but we're at my furrow now and I must get back to work.

There is one last thing I have to ask.

'Amon,' I say. 'What did you tell the others about me back there?'

Amon grins.

'I told them you were just like us Hitler Youth,' he says. 'A boy doing his duty.'

We look at each other for a few moments.

'Thank you,' I say.

Amon clicks his heels together and gives the Nazi salute.

'Heil Richmal,' he says quietly.

I'm late.

The Nazis made us pick potatoes till dark and by the time we were dropped off in the square the town clock was striking six and now I'm hurrying back to the farm as fast as I can.

Genia and Zelda will be frantic.

I have to think what to tell them. Why I've been away all day. I hate lying to them. But I can't tell them the truth, that I'm planning to leave.

What was that?

I stop and peer into the dark trees at the side of the road.

Is somebody following me?

No, it's just my imagination playing tricks. That happens when you have to live with a fake identity and make up untrue stories to tell the people you love.

I start walking again.

'I saw you,' says a voice.

I spin round.

A figure steps out of the trees and comes towards me.

Zelda?

Genia?

The figure steps into a patch of moonlight.

It's Leopold's friend. The kid who shot the soldier. He's still got his gun. He's pointing it at me now.

'I saw you this afternoon,' he says, scowling. 'I saw you talking and grinning with that Hitler Youth vermin.'

I don't know what to say.

I can't take my eyes off the gun.

Up close it looks too big for him. He's only a bit taller than me. But he's holding it in both hands and I know he can use it.

'You're a Nazi vermin spy,' says the kid, aiming the gun at my head.

Then I invited the kid with the gun home for dinner.

He stared at me and I could see from his stunned expression he wasn't sure if he'd heard right.

Dinner?

In the moonlight his dark angry eyes go narrow with suspicion.

His gun wobbles a bit.

I hope I haven't caught him too much by surprise. Some people go twitchy when they're caught by surprise, and Leopold's friend has still got his fingers on the trigger and the gun is still pointing at my head.

I try not to think about what happened last time I saw him point a gun at somebody's head.

The chill breeze is making the autumn leaves rustle in the trees. A leaf floats down near the kid. He sees the movement out of the corner of his eye, swings the gun towards the leaf, realises what it is and points the gun back at me.

He's twitchy all right.

I'll have to be careful.

'Genia's making rabbit stew,' I say, trying to sound relaxed and casual and like I invite people with guns home for dinner every night.

I don't, but this is too good an opportunity to miss.

If I can persuade the kid to stop killing Nazis, the Nazis will do less killings in revenge. Less innocent people hanged from posts. Less chance Zelda could be one of them after I've gone.

'You've met Genia,' I say. 'You helped her plant cabbages. She makes really delicious stew.'

I hope he remembers her. And what a kind person she is.

I'm guessing that a kid who goes round killing Nazis probably doesn't have much in the way of loving grown-ups in his life.

'She'll be really pleased to see a good friend of Leopold's,' I say.

I decide not to tell the kid yet what happened to poor Leopold. No point upsetting a person when you're trying to invite him to dinner.

I can see he's tempted. But he's still frowning.

'Why were you being friendly with that Nazi scum?' he says.

'It's not what you think,' I say. 'His name's Amon and he hates Adolf Hitler as much as we do. He's not like the others.'

The kid still looks doubtful.

'What were you both talking about?' he says.

'Books,' I say. 'Come on. We're late. I'll explain on the way.'

The kid doesn't move.

We stand looking at each other. I have a feeling he wants me to be telling the truth. But there's a world war on and hardly anyone tells the truth in a war.

'After I've explained,' I say, 'if you still think I'm a spy, you can shoot me.'

The kid thinks about this.

'All right,' he says, lowering the gun.

We set off.

'Wilhelm,' shouts Genia as I come into the house. 'Where have you been?'

She's furious.

I have to move fast. If she scares the kid, anything could happen. He's still got the gun in his coat pocket.

'This is Dov,' I say. 'He's a friend of mine. And Leopold's.'

Dov steps uncertainly into the kitchen. Genia stares at him. I can see she's struggling with her feelings. She's still angry with me, but because she's good-hearted she doesn't want to upset a guest.

Zelda is also staring. She hides behind me.

'Children shouldn't play with knives,' she says sternly to Dov.

I don't blame her. The last time she saw Dov he

was threatening her with one. I give her a look to let her know it won't happen this time.

I hope.

'This is Genia,' I say to Dov. 'And Zelda.'

'I'm Violetta, remember?' Zelda hisses.

'It's OK,' I say to her. 'Dov knows about us. He's Jewish.'

Zelda looks at Dov warily. 'So am I,' she says to him. 'Sometimes.'

I glance at Genia to see if she's realised who Dov is. I don't think she has.

'Dov is from the Jewish orphanage,' I say. 'He met Leopold when he was here helping with the cabbages.'

Genia is still staring at him, but with a gentler expression.

'I think I remember you,' she says. 'Hello, Dov.'

'Hello,' he mutters.

'I'm glad you're still alive,' Genia says quietly. 'Where are you living now?'

'Krol's place,' says Dov.

Now it's my turn to stare.

Mr Krol? The turnip man who tried to kidnap me and Zelda?

'Krol rescued you?' says Genia.

Dov nods.

'I thought as much,' she says. 'I had a feeling that sly old grump had someone hidden at his place.'

I try to take this in.

The reward notice on the cart must be just a

disguise, to make the Nazis think Mr Krol hates Jews, so they won't suspect him of protecting one.

Incredible.

'Are you hungry, Dov?' says Genia.

'If there's not enough rabbit stew,' I say to her, 'he can have mine.'

Genia sighs.

'We're not having rabbit stew,' she says. 'We're having cabbage soup again.'

'We caught a rabbit,' says Zelda. 'But I wouldn't let her kill it.'

Genia gives me and Zelda an exasperated look. Sort of loving and cross at the same time. Like she's forgiving us but wondering where it will all end.

'Sorry there's no stew,' Zelda says to Dov.

'That's all right,' he says gruffly.

'I'm sure Dov understands,' says Genia to Zelda. 'If he's friends with Felix, he probably doesn't like the idea of killing things either.'

After we have the soup, Zelda shows Dov her drawings.

'This is Violetta's mummy and daddy being nice to chickens,' she says.

While Dov looks at the drawings, I try to think of a way of persuading him to stop killing Nazis.

As it turns out, I don't need to.

Genia is sweeping up. Dov's coat is on the floor where he left it. Genia moves it to sweep under it and the gun falls out with a clatter.

We all look at the gun.

Nobody says anything.

Dov just stares at the table and sort of hunches his shoulders.

Genia picks the gun up and puts it back in Dov's coat pocket. I can see she's thinking hard. When I got back from the river, I told her about seeing Leopold's friend shoot a Nazi. I think she's guessed that's who Dov is.

She comes and sits next to Dov at the kitchen table. Before she can say anything, he turns to her angrily.

'I came here to see Leopold,' he says. 'Where's Leopold?'

Genia hesitates.

This is the moment I've been dreading. I should have told Dov about Leopold on the way here, but I was worried he wouldn't want to come.

'Don't you know anything?' says Zelda quietly. 'The Nazis killed Leopold.'

Dov jumps to his feet.

I do too. For a second I think he's going to lash out at Zelda. But instead he just looks at Genia as if he's pleading with her to say it's not true.

Genia looks at him and nods sadly.

Dov grabs a wooden bowl and hurls it across the room. It bangs against the wall near the shelf. I hold my breath and wait for Genia to get angry. The bowl almost hit the photo of her husband.

She doesn't.

She just takes hold of Dov's hand and gently pulls him back down onto the bench next to her.

'We all miss Leopold a lot,' she says. 'Just like you must miss your parents. They used to run the Jewish orphanage, didn't they?'

Dov doesn't say anything. Just stares at the table.

'Felix and Zelda miss their families an awful lot,' Genia says quietly. 'I miss my sister and her children. We know how you feel, Dov.'

Dov is clenching his teeth, like he doesn't want to let any words out. But he does.

'No you don't,' he mutters.

Genia slowly reaches across the table and slides a clean piece of paper over in front of Dov. She puts the pencil on top of it.

'Show us,' she says softly.

For a long time Dov just sits there, staring at the paper.

Just when I think he's not going to touch it, he suddenly picks up the pencil and starts drawing. Not with careful little movements like Zelda does when she draws. With big violent slashes. Sometimes he tears the paper, but he keeps going.

Me and Zelda and Genia watch.

He's drawing a pit in the ground. I recognise what it is. The children's grave. There are lots of people lying in it and lots of people standing next to it and lots of Nazis shooting them.

A drop of liquid splashes onto the paper.

It's a tear.

Dov wipes his face with his hand.

'They took us into the forest,' he says, his teeth still clenched. 'Me and my mum and my dad and my brother and all the orphan kids. They shot us. We fell into the hole. I wasn't dead. People fell on top of me. I was buried in people. They were moaning. They stopped moaning. I climbed out. It was dark. I looked for my family. There were too many bodies.'

Dov drops the pencil onto the table and puts his hands over his face. His whole body is shaking.

'I couldn't find them,' he sobs.

Genia puts her arms round him and holds him tight.

We're all crying now, Genia included.

After a while, Zelda wipes her eyes. She picks up the pencil and starts drawing on a fresh piece of paper. When she's finished, she goes round to the other side of the table and gives the drawing to Dov.

I lean over to see what she's drawn.

It's very simple.

Two grown-ups with their arms round a child.

'This is my mummy and daddy,' says Zelda to Dov quietly. 'They're Nazis. They're saying sorry.'

Then it was time for Dov to leave. Genia went with him to Mr Krol's place to make sure he got there safely. I stayed at the kitchen table with Zelda.

She did another drawing.

Two grown-ups and a child. And some chickens. All dancing.

'This is me and my mummy and daddy,' says Zelda. 'We're not Jewish, but we still love each other.'

I smile at her.

'I'm glad,' I say. 'I'm glad you're not cross with your mummy and daddy any more.'

Zelda is looking sadly at the picture.

'They couldn't help being Nazis,' she says quietly. 'I couldn't tell them not to, I was too little.'

I give Zelda a hug.

After a long time she lifts her face from my neck and looks at me with a serious expression.

'Felix,' she says. 'Tell Leopold's friend I don't want to shoot Nazis any more.'

I smile again. I'm so happy for her and not just because she'll be safer now. When your mum and dad have been killed, it's even worse if you're angry with them.

I go to my coat and get Zelda's locket. I put it round her neck.

'Will you wear this now?' I say. 'To keep you safe?'

Zelda opens the locket and looks at the little photo of her parents.

She frowns.

'You keep me safe,' she says. 'And Genia does. And Richmal Crompton does.'

'We try to,' I say. 'But wearing this will help keep you even safer. It'll make the Nazis like you.'

She thinks about this for a long time.

'Even if the other Nazis do like me,' she says, 'I won't like them.'

But she leaves the locket on.

'Thank you,' I say.

'I'm going to do some more drawings,' says Zelda, picking up the pencil again. 'I'm going to do one now of when my mummy cooked me an egg.'

I give her another smile, but suddenly I'm full of sadness.

I know why. It's nearly time for me to go.

Zelda looks at me, concerned.

'It's all right,' she says. 'My mummy's cooking you an egg too.'

I think about how lucky I am to have Zelda, and

that makes my sadness even stronger. But it's not time to go just yet.

While Zelda draws more pictures, I write a story. It's a long story about the things the Nazis have done to my family and Dov's family and all the other people they've hurt too.

When I've finished, me and Zelda go out to the barn.

Leopold's kennel is covering the hole I dug in the barn floor. I drag it to one side.

'What are you doing?' says Zelda.

I jump down into the hole and fold my story into a small square of paper and push it into the soft earth.

'I'm hiding my story,' I explain. 'When the war's over and the Nazis have been defeated, it will be evidence of what they did.'

Zelda thinks about this.

'Who's going to make them defeated?' she asks.

'The English,' I say.

I tell Zelda what Genia told me one time. How the English have still got an army and one day they're going to attack the Nazis.

'You mean Richmal Crompton?' says Zelda.

'She'll help,' I say.

Zelda kneels by the hole and hands me down some crumpled pieces of paper.

'Hide my evidence too,' she says. 'So Richmal Crompton's army will know that my mummy and daddy weren't bad Nazis.'

I look at the pieces of paper. They're her drawings of her parents dancing and cooking her an egg and bathing her knee when she cut it.

I fold the drawings and push them into the soil next to my story.

Zelda helps me scramble out of the hole and we brush the dirt off my trousers. While we do, I tell her about Amon, the Hitler Youth boy. I tell her how she must ask for him if she ever gets into trouble with the Nazis.

She stops brushing and looks at me.

'What about you?' she says. 'Why don't I ask for you?'

I take a deep breath.

'This is in case something happens to me and I'm not here,' I say.

Zelda puts her arms round my waist and hugs me tight.

'Nothing's going to happen to you,' she says. 'I'm not going to let it. Don't you know anything?'

Genia gets home and we all go to bed and I sleep the whole night with my arms round Zelda.

Not the whole night.

I wake up before dawn.

Was that a noise outside? I listen carefully. I have a fleeting thought that it's Dov creeping around out there in the farmyard, but it's probably just part of a dream I was having.

All I can hear is the wind.

I know this is the time I should go.

Genia and Zelda are both asleep. I should creep out now and leave them the note I've written telling them how much safer they'll be without me and how I promise I'll come back after the war and find them.

But I can't.

I just want to stay here a little bit longer.

I'll go in a while, before they wake up.

Then I opened my eyes again and Genia was gently shaking me.

'Wilhelm, wake up.'

I stare at her, confused. I fumble for my glasses and put them on. Genia's up and dressed. I must have slept in. Zelda appears next to her, up and dressed too.

'Mr Krol's giving us a ride into town,' says Zelda. 'To get you a birthday present.'

I'm even more confused.

It's November. My birthday isn't until January.

Genia and Zelda are both grinning at me. Genia holds my Wilhelm identity card close to my face and points to where it says *Date Of Birth*.

29 November, 1931.

'Today's the twenty-ninth,' says Genia. 'You're eleven today. Happy birthday, Wilhelm.'

I try to sit up. Genia gently but firmly pushes me back down into bed.

'You have to stay here,' she says. 'It's a surprise. I'm not using my last three eggs on a present if it's not going to be a surprise. Anyway, you need to rest and get better.' She strokes the bruise on my head. 'Promise me you won't go out playing like yesterday.'

'I promise,' I say quietly.

It's true. Travelling to another part of Poland and finding a place to hide isn't playing.

'See you later, birthday boy,' says Genia.

I sit up and throw my arms round her.

'Thank you,' I say, struggling not to cry. 'Thank you for looking after me and Zelda.'

Genia gives me a long hug.

'Thank you,' she whispers. 'I was turning into a miserable old turnip before you two came along.'

She stands up and goes out.

Zelda has gone out too.

I panic.

Before I can jump out of bed, Zelda runs back in, putting her coat on. She jumps up onto the bed, kisses me on the cheek, and jumps down again.

She stops in the doorway and turns to me with a grin.

'Happy birthday,' she says.

Then she's gone.

I don't hang around.

I have to keep busy.

If I stop and get sad I won't be able to do it.

I get up and put all my clothes on. My trousers

and coat and boots and both shirts and all my socks.

I put the note on the kitchen table and write an extra bit thanking Genia and Zelda for the surprise birthday present whatever it is and asking them to keep it safe for me till I come back after the war.

Halfway to the door I stop and go back to the table and find a clean piece of paper and write something else.

The story of Zelda and Genia and their loving hearts.

It's the most important story I've ever written and it's very easy to write because it's already come true.

I'm going to hide it in the barn with the other evidence. So the whole world will know. In case something happens and I don't come back.

I drag Leopold's kennel off the hiding hole in the barn.

And almost faint with shock.

There's a man in the hole.

He's lying there on some straw. He's wearing a ragged suit and blinking up at me like he's been asleep.

He sits up and raises his arms like I'm going to attack him. But when he sees I'm just a kid he lowers them.

'Who are you?' he says.

'Felix,' I say. 'I mean Wilhelm.'

He looks at me for a long time.

I wonder if I should be running. Is he going to grab me for the reward? I think if he was, he would have done it by now. Plus he wouldn't have a kind face like this man.

He's nodding to himself.

'Now I understand,' he says.

I wish I did.

'I'm Gabriek,' says the man, standing up in the hole. 'Genia's husband. I got here in the middle of the night. When I looked through the window and saw somebody in bed with my wife, I . . .'

He doesn't finish the sentence, but I know what he's trying to say. In wartime, with people being killed every day, a lot of people end up in bed married to other people's husbands and wives.

'I decided to wait till morning,' says Gabriek. 'To find out who this person was and . . .'

'It was me,' I say. 'And Zelda. Genia's been protecting us.'

Best to get it out in the open straight off. So we both know where we stand.

Gabriek is nodding to himself again.

'I'm not surprised,' he says. 'My wife has a very big heart.'

I agree with him as he climbs out of the hole.

'Is she awake?' he says.

I explain how Genia's gone into town with Zelda.

'I'm sorry she's not here,' I say. 'It's sort of my

fault. They've gone to get me a birthday present.'

Gabriek is looking sad.

But he still wishes me a happy birthday.

Later, after I've explained everything to Gabriek and he's read all the evidence in the hole and seen my note and examined Zelda's pictures, he looks at me, concerned.

'It's nearly winter,' he says, 'Where are you planning to go? Back to the Catholic orphanage?'

I shake my head.

'If I go to there,' I say, 'I'll be putting Mother Minka and the others in danger. I have to find somewhere I can hide on my own.'

Gabriek frowns as he thinks about this.

'I can't tell you what you should do, Felix,' he says. 'If you want to stay here with us, I'll do everything I can to protect you. But the final decision has to be yours.'

'Thank you,' I say.

What a brave and kind man. I can see why Genia chose him to marry. But his kindness has put my mind in a whirl.

I jump down into the hole and busily hide the evidence again, partly to give myself a chance to think.

Could Gabriek still protect Zelda if the Nazis discovered my private part? He'd have Amon to help him, but would that be enough? Or would he and Genia and Zelda all be killed for sheltering me?

I so much want to stay.

But the more I think about it, the more I know, for their sakes, I have to go.

Suddenly I see something glinting under the straw in the bottom of the hole. I pick it up.

Zelda's locket.

Her good protection.

She must have left it here last night as part of her evidence.

She's in town now, without it.

Now I know I definitely have to go, and quickly.

I must get it to her.

Then I said goodbye to Gabriek and ran into town, Zelda's locket hard and hot in my fist.

Oh no.

The town is already crowded.

It's market day. How will I find Zelda and Genia in among all these people?

I can only think of one place to start looking.

Cyryl's shop.

I push my way along the street, trying not to go too close to the groups of Nazi soldiers bullying the stallholders for bargains.

'Hey, Jewboy.'

I freeze.

You know how when you're in a crowd and there's one person you don't want to bump into and you suddenly hear his voice yelling at you and it feels like a bad dream?

That's happening to me now.

But it's not a dream.

Cyryl is pushing his way towards me, wet lips smirking.

'Your Hitler Youth friends can't help you now, Jewboy,' he says. 'The police have arrested your vermin family.'

I stare at him, panic and confusion like a huge noisy crowd in my head.

'Your stupid aunty and your stupid sister turned up at our shop with that Jew-lover Krol,' says Cyryl. 'The Nazis have had suspicions about him for ages. So when he walked in this morning and tried to buy clothes for a boy, my mother called the police.'

Dread slices into my guts like a bayonet.

'That aunty of yours is a thug,' says Cyryl. 'She hit my mother. And your vermin sister bit a soldier. The Nazi police had to drag them away.'

'Where did they take them?' I say.

Cyryl does a big wet grin.

'Town square,' he says.

The town square is packed with people but I see Mr Krol straight away.

Oh.

Oh no.

Then I see Zelda and Genia.

I pray it's not really them. I pray that any second they'll come up behind me and give me a hug and Zelda will tell me off for having smudgy glasses and not being able see clearly.

She won't.

Because I can see clearly. Even with smudged glasses. Even with tears.

Oh Zelda.

Oh Genia.

The breeze turns them gently and now they're facing me.

Please, Richmal Crompton, do something.

If I go over there and lift them down from those posts and take those ropes from round their necks, it's not too late is it?

I close my eyes because I know it is too late.

I can't move.

I'm numb.

All I want to do is stay numb for ever. So I just stand here until some Nazi soldiers tell me to get lost and shove me away.

Then I'm not numb any more.

Then all I want to do is kill.

Then I went to Mr Krol's farm.

No sign of Dov in the house.

I call his name while I look for a cellar or an attic or a hole in the barn floor. Finally I find him in the turnip bunker.

I tell him what's happened and what I want to do.

He doesn't take it in at first. He's too busy staring at the wall and swearing and throwing turnips and crying and going on about what a good person Mr Krol was.

I tell him again.

'I want to kill as many of them as I can,' I say.

Dov looks at me.

This time he gets it.

He reaches under some turnips and pulls out a bag and unzips it.

I've seen that bag before.

'All right,' says Dov. 'Let's do it.'

Then we did the planning and the preparations, and then we went to get our revenge.

I should be scared, I know.

We walk towards the Nazi orphanage through the darkness. The big house ahead of us is all lit up. I can see guards at the gates. Soldiers and officers strutting around inside. All with guns. All trained to fight. And Hitler Youth vermin who say they'll protect innocent kids but don't.

I should be scared, but I'm not.

All I'm thinking about is how many of them I can kill. And how many of their families I can hurt. Families suffer a lot when fathers and sons are blown to pieces. Sometimes they go mad. Sometimes they starve.

Good.

'Slow down,' hisses Dov.

I know what he's worried about. Us looking suspicious. Or slipping in the snow and going sprawling and showing the Nazis what we've got hidden under our coats.

I slow down.

We stroll up to the main gate. Dov says hello to the guard in German. The guard looks at us.

The blood on our Hitler Youth uniforms is on the back so the guard can't see it. Dov was clever, shooting them that way.

The guard says something to us and waves us in.

We stroll through the gate, trying not to look too fat. It's not easy when you've got six grenades taped to your chest and tummy.

My coat starts to slip off my shoulders and I yank it back on. I need it in position, partly to disguise the fatness and partly because of the other grenade in the side pocket.

The one I'll explode first.

The one that will make all the others on my chest explode.

We reach the house. Dov looks at me. I look at him. This is where we split up. Him in the front. Me in the back. Two human bombs in two different parts of the house.

That way we'll kill more of them.

Dov isn't crying now. His eyes are hard. Mine are too. He doesn't say anything. Neither do I. There's nothing to say.

Dov goes up the front steps.

I hurry round to the back of the house. I find

an open door. Inside is a corridor. I go down it, listening for voices.

I want lots of voices.

I want a room packed with Nazis.

A thought hits me. What if Dov explodes himself before me? What if the Nazis in this part of the building all run away before I can blow them up?

I grip the grenade in my pocket, my finger through the ring of the pin.

Yes.

Voices.

I push open a door. A room full of Nazis. Some of them turn and stare at me. I hesitate. They're mostly Hitler Youth.

Doesn't matter.

I start to pull the pin.

'Wilhelm.'

A voice behind me.

Dov?

I stop. I turn.

It's Amon. He's staring at me, his face all upset. Does he know? Has he guessed what I'm here to do?

'Wilhelm,' he says in a strange voice. 'Come. I have your book.'

He grabs my shoulders and steers me back out into the corridor. I start to pull the pin again.

I hesitate again.

There's something about Amon's expression. He's not looking scared, he's looking sad. Plus he's closed the door behind us. Now it's just him and me in the corridor.

'I tried, Wilhelm,' he says. 'I tried to save your sister but they wouldn't listen to me.'

He's holding something up in front of my face. Something that glitters in the corridor lights.

'This was in your sister's coat,' he says. 'Wilhelm, I'm sorry.'

I take it from him.

A locket.

Not silver like Zelda's. A gold one.

It's open. Inside each half is a tiny drawing. A boy on one side, a girl on the other. They're facing each other. Under the girl is the letter Z. Under the boy is the letter F.

I stare at it.

My birthday present.

I stare at it for a long time.

Then I take my hand off the grenade in my pocket.

Then I grabbed Amon and dragged him down the corridor towards the back door.

'What are you doing?' he says.

I don't answer.

As we burst out into the night, a huge explosion smashes through the house.

Screams.

Frantic shouting.

Rubble falling.

I realise I'm lying on the ground with pain in my ears and gravel in my mouth.

I find my glasses and put them on. They're cracked, but I can still see.

Amon is on the ground too, staring at me in shock.

All around us, chaos.

Dust.

Panic.

People staggering around.

I pull the unexploded grenades off my chest and wriggle out of what's left of the Hitler Youth uniform.

Amon is saying something, but I can't hear what. I see the Richmal Crompton book I gave him, sticking out of his pocket.

I take it.

I still don't speak.

I get to my feet.

I run.

Then I came back here to the barn and climbed into the hiding hole and pulled the kennel over me and I've been here ever since.

Nearly eleven months.

The Nazis didn't come looking for me so I think Amon must have told them I was blown up with Dov. If he did, I'm grateful to him.

I'm even more grateful to Gabriek.

He brings me food once a night and takes my wees and poos away and washes me sometimes and we have very good talks and sometimes we read Richmal Crompton stories to each other.

He always calls me Felix.

Sometimes we talk about Genia, which makes us sad but also happy because of how lucky we were to have her.

My legs are a bit weak and so are my eyes. I don't get to use them much here in my dark hiding place.

But my memory is strong.

I've kept it strong by telling the story of me and Zelda in my head as I lie here on the straw. It's what I do all day. It's how I'm keeping my promise to Zelda. It's why I decided to live.

I'm Zelda's evidence.

She helps me. She stays in my mind all the time. I don't even have to ask her.

One day in the future, when Richmal Crompton's army defeats the Nazis, I'll climb out of here and be the best human being I can for the rest of my life.

To show people what Zelda was like.

'She was only six,' I'll say, 'but she had the loving heart of a ten-year-old.'

And if people carry on hating each other and killing each other and being cruel to each other, I'll tell them something else.

'You can be like her,' I'll say. 'Don't you know anything?'

Let's see what they do then.

Dear Reader,

As with Once *(the first book I wrote about Felix and Zelda), this story comes from my imagination, but it was inspired by a period of history that was all too real.*

I couldn't have written this story without first reading many books about the Holocaust. Books full of the voices of the real people who lived and struggled and loved and died and, just a few of them, survived in that terrible time.

I also read about the generosity and bravery of the people who risked their lives to shelter others, often children who were not members of their family or faith, and by doing so saved them.

You can find a list of these books on my website. I hope you get to read some of them and help keep alive the memory of those people.

This story is my imagination trying to grasp the unimaginable.

Their stories are the real stories.

Morris Gleitzman
June 2008

morrisgleitzman.com
puffin.co.uk